Fellowship Farm 5

Books 13-15

Melanie Lotfali

JUNIOR YOUTH CAN MOVE THE WORLD

FLYING FITZGERALDS

FLOOD ON FELLOWSHIP FARM

BOOK THIRTEEN

JUNIOR YOUTH CAN MOVE THE WORLD

In the thirteenth book of the Fellowship Farm series, the Fitzgerald family learn that service can sometimes be fun, and sometimes be boring, cold, and difficult. Leezah has many opportunities to develop her courage, and the family say a teary goodbye to a dear friend.

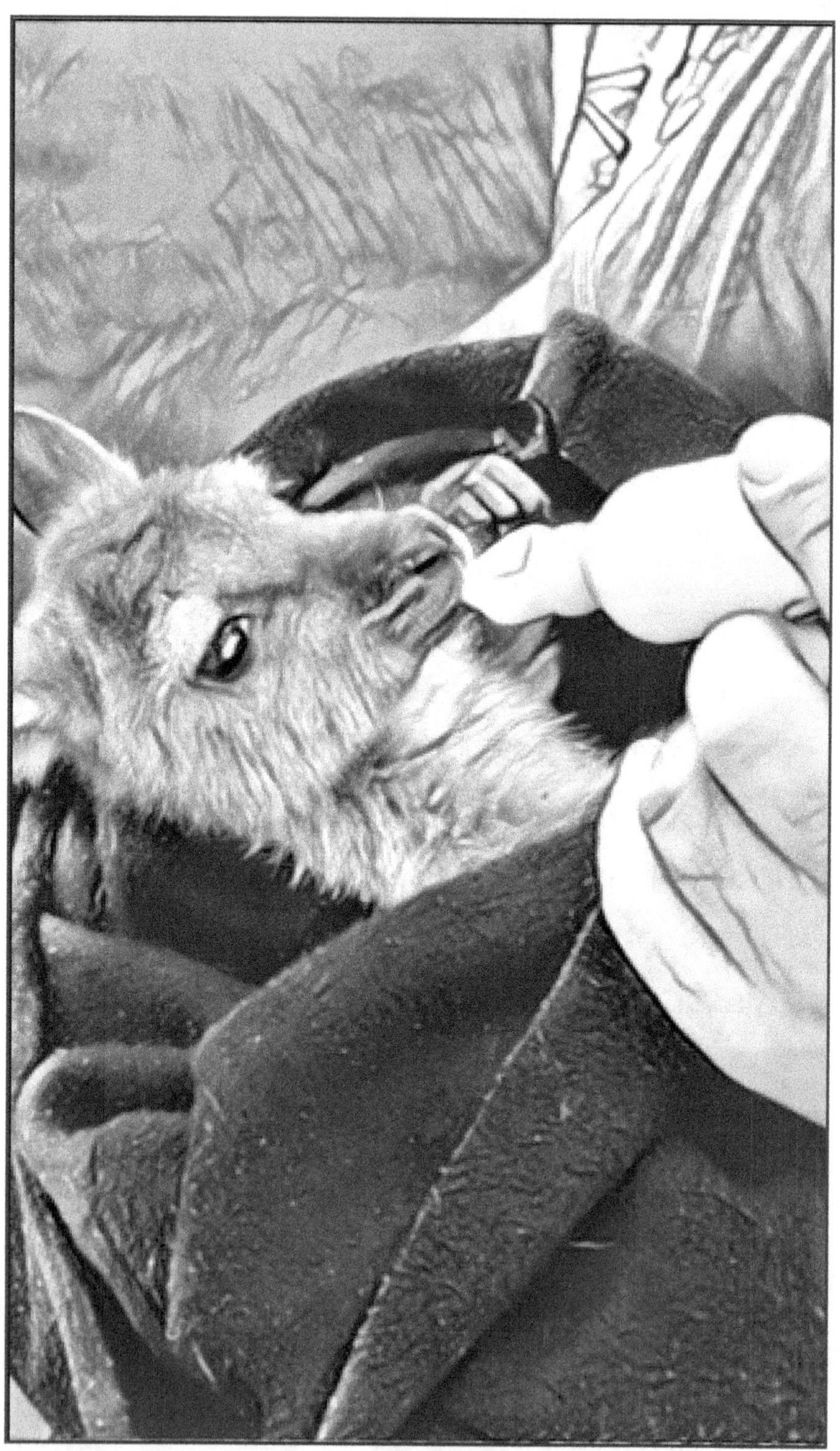

Feeding Joey

It wasn't even five o'clock but the sun had set on Fellowship Farm. The winter air was icy. Seven-year-old Olingah Fitzgerald shivered in the boot room at the back of the farmhouse. He put on his warm coat, woollen hat and yellow gumboots. When he was dressed, he picked up a large glass bottle with a big black rubber teat on the end. His mother, Rommy had filled it with warm Wombaroo milk.

The outside lights shone on the path that lead from the back garden, down the side of the house to the front 'garden'. Out the back, just visible in the setting sun was a large patch of lawn edged on three sides by rose beds and a fence. To the right was a large cage full of pigeons, now sleeping on their perches. Between the pigeons and the house was a large, brightly painted dog house.

Inside the dog house were three 8-month old puppies, Flea, Flex and Fizz. When they heard Olingah, they came scuttling out of their house and galloping up the lawn and steps to greet him.

Normally Olingah would have loved to play with them, but he had an important job to do. He also didn't want to drop the bottle of Wombaroo milk. So with one hand he patted their bobbing heads, and gently pushed them away. Olingah carefully slid open the wooden barrier that temporarily separated the back garden from the front garden. He squeezed himself through as quickly as he could without letting the puppies through. Then he pulled the barrier closed.

The puppies stood on the other side, tongues out, wagging their tails. Their panting breath made fumes of steam in the cold air. "Go back to bed, you silly gooses," said Olingah with a smile, and clomped down the side of the house.

At the front, hanging on an old fence post, was a 'pouch'. The pouch was made of a bag, lined with old woollen jumpers which were covered in old cotton pillow cases. As Olingah approached, a large joey pulled itself out of the pouch and moved slowly toward Olingah. Olingah hid the bottle behind his back. The wallaby knew exactly why Olingah was there and it started to snuffle at Olingah's waist and stretch its head around to Olingah's back. Olingah giggled as the joey nudged at him. "Good determination, Joey!" he said, nearly toppling over.

Olingah brought the bottle to the front of his body and tipped it up so the teat was facing the mouth of the wallaby. The wallaby immediately began to gobble the milk. Olingah had to hold on tightly to the bottle.

Nearly one month earlier, the Fitzgerald family had rescued the wallaby from the side of the road. Its mother had been hit by a car. It was already quite big when its mother was killed. Rommy, who was the town vet, thought the wallaby was probably about nine months old now.

The family was reducing the number of milk feeds. The wallaby was now given milk only once in the morning and once at night. It was also given some pellet food. But it was free to move around the front garden and eat the grass and other plants growing there. Soon it would be time to take it up to the back paddock and set it free into the bush. Olingah really didn't want to do that. He loved feeding the wallaby with the special milk, and watching it move around the overgrown front garden.

When the wallaby had finished all the milk, it kept butting the bottle and sucking, hoping for more. It always seemed to be hungry. "That's all for tonight, Joey," said Olingah. He pulled the teat from the wallaby's mouth. "You'll have to get your own food from the garden now."

It seemed like the wallaby understood Olingah's words. He turned aside and slowly lolloped toward the long grass growing near the front gate. Olingah went inside to join his family.

Inside the farmhouse Olingah's father, Flip, had lit the fire in the living room. The flames were blazing in the fire place, sparks flew up the chimney and the dry wood crackled. Leezah and Skye-Maree were changing out of their farm clothes. The three children had just finished the farm chores before Olingah went to feed the wallaby. They put on clean warm tracksuit pants, skivvies, jumpers, and woolly socks. Olingah did the same.

Rommy had arrived home from her veterinary surgery just in time to make up the

Wombaroo milk. When Olingah came back into the house she was also changing out of her work clothes into some warm and comfortable house clothes.

Flip had been on the farm all day. He was dirty and sweaty. So he took his shower and put on his warm pyjamas before dinner. The children could hear him singing loudly. "I'm siiiiiiinging in the rain. Just siiiiinging in the rain. What a glooooooorious feeling. I'm ha ha happy again." This was followed by a loud gurgling sound.

Soon afterward Flip came out of his bedroom in his flannelette pyjamas and dressing gown. On his feet were Ugg boots made of sheepskin. His damp hair was sticking straight up.

Olingah was wiping and setting the dining table in the living room. In the kitchen, Leezah was chopping potatoes. Skye-Maree was chopping carrots and Rommy was cutting meat into small strips. On the stove, a pot with frying onion was sizzling. This pot would soon be full of the ingredients for the stew. As Flip walked through the living room, he heard Olingah talking to himself while he worked.

"Fork on the left. Knife on the right. Bowl in the middle. Napkin on the left. Glass on the right." When he saw his father, Olingah started to laugh.

"What's up doc?" asked Flip.

"Your hair Daddy!" replied Olingah.

"You're just jealous," said Flip with wide eyes and a serious face.

"You look like a galah!" Olingah chuckled.

"Oh no! You have discovered my secret identity!" With a loud galah-like screech, Flip flapped his arms and swooped on Olingah, wrapping him in a big hug and lifting him off his feet. "Don't tell anyone," he whispered with a wink, as he lowered his son back down in front of the table, and went into the kitchen to help prepare dinner.

When dinner was ready, the Fitzgerald family sat up at the table. Before they started to eat, Skye-Maree said, "I was reading a book about a family who lived by a beach. There were two children – called Joy and Lee. Before every meal, they would always say a little prayer. I really like it. I was thinking we could say it before we eat too?"

"Sounds great darling," said Rommy. "Why don't you say it for us tonight?"

Everyone closed their eyes and bowed their heads, in reverence.

Skye said, "May we eat this food with thanks and use its energy to help all beings live together in peace, love, joy, and harmony."

After a few seconds of silence, the family started to eat.

"Yum!" said Olingah.

"What a beautiful prayer," said Flip.

"What's the book called?" asked Leezah.

"It's called The Island of Indirrah. It's really good. The children keep wishing they could turn into mermaids. They wish on everything – shooting stars, birthday candles, all sorts of things. And then a day comes when they have made the same wish one thousand times. At that moment they turn into mermaids. They have all sorts of adventures under the sea. And in the end..."

"They get eaten by a shark?" suggested Flip

"Don't tell me!" said Leezah, "I want to read it!"

The warm stew with crusty buttered buns was delicious. The fire heated the living room. The Fitzgeralds shared news of their day at work and school. Then Olingah said, "Dad, what's in this stew?"

"The usual Olly. Spiders' eyes, snakes' tongues, mouldy cheese, a sprinkling of flies, and fur balls of cat."

"Daaaaaddy!" said Olingah. "Mum, what's in the stew?"

"Onions, carrots, potatoes and meat," replied Rommy.

"What kind of meat?" asked Olingah.

"Tonight we are having kangaroo meat. But sometimes we make stew with lamb, beef, or chicken."

Slowly Olingah stopped eating. He seemed lost in deep thought. And he looked a little worried. His bowl was still half full. By the time everyone else finished their stew and their bread rolls Olingah's bowl was still half full.

"Have you had enough to eat, possum?" asked Flip. The family always stayed at the table until everyone had finished their meal, so they were all waiting for Olingah. He didn't answer the question. Instead he pushed his bowl away and said, "So, what's the difference between the kangaroo we are eating and the wallaby we are taking care of?"

Setting a noble goal

With a nod from Rommy, Leezah and Skye-Maree started to clear the table. Rommy and Flip sat with Olingah.

"There's not really any difference," said Rommy slowly, answering Olingah's question.

Olingah's eyes widened and started to fill with tears. His chest felt tight. His tummy felt like it was being tied in knots.

"So that means that eating kangaroo stew is like eating Joey?"

Rommy paused. Then she said, "Well, yes Olly. In a way, it is."

"And eating chicken is like eating Kanga Rooster," said Olingah, referring to the pet rooster the family had bought from Kellyton markets.

"Well, yes."

"But that's terrible!" said Olingah. Tears started to run from his eyes, and his nose started running too. Flip passed him a tissue. "I would never eat Joey or Kanga Rooster!"

Olingah was starting to sob. He wondered why he had never thought about it before.

"What's the difference between eating a cow and eating the cows we feed every day? What's the difference between eating lamb and eating Flea, Flex, and Fizz?" he sobbed.

"Well, Olly, it's true. They are all animals. And they all have the same feelings."

Olingah sat for a long while thinking about what he had just realised. Gradually his tears stopped flowing. He leaned his elbows on the table and rested his chin in his hands. He closed his eyes. Rommy and Flip looked at each other. They decided to leave Olly to think, and they went to help the girls in the kitchen.

When Olingah opened his eyes again the table was clear and the kitchen was tidy. Leezah, Skye, and Rommy were having showers. Flip was reading on the couch by the fire. Olingah felt very tired. He left the table and went to sit on the couch with his dad. He leaned against Flip's shoulder and Flip stroked

Olly's head. "I never ever want to eat meat again Daddy," Olingah said quietly.

"Ok possum. Done. No more meat for Olly," said Flip. They sat quietly together watching the fire crackle and flame.

"And I think we should all stop eating meat," added Olingah.

"Mmmm, let's consult about that," suggested Flip. "When everyone's finished their showers we can have a family consultation."

Olingah nodded. Flip stood up and went to the book case. He pulled out a Bahá'í book called Lights of Guidance. Olingah went to get his pyjamas and have a shower.

When Rommy, Leezah, Skye-Maree and Olingah joined Flip in the living room they were happy to find five steaming mugs of hot chocolate. Flip had heated a big pot of milk and added lots of honey and cocoa powder. They each took a mug and sat on the floor or couches by the fire. Neither Leezah nor Skye had any homework, so each of them was planning to read until bedtime. Skye was reading Prince Caspian and Leezah was reading A Wrinkle in Time. When everyone was settled, and had started sipping their drinks, Flip said, "Nice chocolate milk moustaches everyone! And, more importantly, we would like to have a family consultation." He looked at Olingah. It was getting close to Olingah's bedtime and he was feeling quite sleepy. But Olingah said, "I would like to let you know I am not going to eat meat ever again. I don't think it is kind or just or helpful or friendly."

"Or compassionate," added Leezah.

"Yes," said Olingah, "or compassionate. And I would like to suggest we all practice our compassionate and kindness."

"Practice our compassion by not eating meat Olly?" asked Rommy.

"Yes," said Olingah.

Flip read from Lights of Guidance. "'Abdul'-Bahá says 'the food of man is cereals and fruit...he is not in need of meat... Even without eating meat he would live with the utmost vigour and energy... the killing of animals and the eating of their meat is somewhat contrary to pity and compassion, and if one can content oneself with cereals, fruit, oil and nuts, such as pistachios, almonds and so on, it would undoubtedly be better and more pleasing.'"

"So no more bacon? No more sausages? No more roasts? Nor more ham sandwiches? No more hamburgers on the barbecue?" asked Skye-Maree.

Olly hadn't thought of all those things. He loved bacon and eggs on the weekends, and barbecues on Holy Days. His voice was a little wobbly as he said "Nooope. No more." But then he remembered Joey, Kanga, Flea, Flex, Fizz, and Bonnie the horse. "No more meat," he said more firmly.

"It makes sense," said Leezah.

"What will we eat instead?" asked Skye-Maree.

"Chocolate?" suggested Flip.

Skye's face lit up.

"Pipe down pipsqueak!" said Rommy to Flip and crossed her eyes at him. "We could do an experiment for a month," she suggested. "We could see how we go. We've read the guidance of `Abdul'-Bahá. We've had some consultation. Now we can take action. Then we can reflect. That's how the Universal House of Justice tells us to learn about anything. Study, consult, act, reflect."

Everyone agreed to the experiment. As soon as the consultation finished, Flip reached for the guitar and the family sang some evening prayers. Then Olingah went straight off to bed without being reminded.

Leezah leaned against Rommy's chair, while Rommy plaited Leezah's thick curls. Leezah was half reading, half thinking. She was thinking about the junior youth group that was meeting in two days' time. At Naw Ruz Leezah had decided to form a junior youth group. There were no junior youth group animators in Kellyton. A young woman called Ruha came from Limedale every two weeks, on Saturday afternoons, to run the group. Leezah invited six of her friends from school to join the group, and three of them joined.

Ruha was accompanying some youth from Kellyton who were learning to become animators, so they also joined the sessions. So every second Saturday afternoon, four junior youth and three youth met at Fellowship Farm for the Junior Youth Spiritual Empowerment

Programme. Skye-Maree and Olingah desperately wanted to join the group. They begged and begged to be allowed to join. But Rommy said that the junior youth group was only for junior youth.

The group had met six times. It was studying Breezes of Confirmation. Leezah thought to herself that Olingah had just experienced confirmation. He set himself a noble goal – to not eat animals – and by the end of the evening the whole family had agreed to try being vegetarians.

On Saturday the junior youth group was going to start its first service project. Leezah was very excited about it.

Service and joy

On Saturday afternoon at two o'clock Ruha arrived at Fellowship Farm with her van full of junior youth and youth. Leezah, Skye-Maree, and Olingah were waiting at the front gate when the van drove in. Ruha was eighteen years old. She had already finished school. She had brown skin, red cheeks, sparkly eyes and curly hair. As soon as she stepped out of the car her face lit up in a radiant smile and she embraced all three Fitzgeralds at once in a big hug. Ruha had moved from Tonga to Tasmania to live for a year while she did her youth year of service. She loved Leezah, Skye, and Olly, and they adored her. Leezah wanted to be just like Ruha when she grew up.

The rest of the junior youth and youth tumbled out of the van and headed in to the house. The junior youth group met in the sunroom at the front of the house so they all walked through the kitchen and living room, down the hall to the sunroom. Olingah and Skye-Maree followed. They hoped that if they sat quietly as mice, no one would notice them. The group sat in a circle for prayers.

"Lovely to have you with us Olly and Skye," said Ruha warmly.

Olly and Skye sat reverently, hoping that the prayers would start and they would be able to stay. Then Rommy appeared at the door of the sunroom. Ruha grinned up at Rommy and down at the bowed heads.

"Olly. Skye. Wonderful reverence but let's practice obedience!! Time to take Flea, Flex, and Fizz for a walk."

Olly and Skye sloped out of the room, wishing desperately that they could be junior youth. Skye still had two years but Olly had another four! Rommy pulled the sunroom door shut behind them.

Ruha reached for the guitar that Leezah had taken to the sunroom earlier. Ruha's fingers on the strings seemed to create magic. They made the most beautiful sounds come from the guitar. Ruha's beautiful voice also brought the prayers to life. It was easy to be reverent when listening to Ruha sing. The junior youth sang the quotes they had already learned in the group. "Regard man as a mine rich in gems of inestimable value," they sang enthusiastically. And "Let your heart burn with loving kindness for all who may cross your path."

Then Ruha spread a big piece of yellow card in the middle of the group. She asked each of them to think about the word service. She asked them to think about the question, "What is service?" She handed out felt pens, crayons, coloured paper, scissors and glue. She asked them to answer the question by writing, drawing, or using collage.

Leezah wrote the word "FUN" in the middle of the card and surrounded it by balloons cut out of coloured paper. Someone else wrote the word "sometimes" in front of what Leezah had written and also "sometimes not." Someone else drew a picture of children washing their mum's car. One of the youth wrote "Service is thinking of others" and drew lots of thought bubbles with pictures of people in them.

Soon the card was covered in words and pictures. When they had finished, Ruha stuck a piece of paper along the bottom of the card.

It said "Service to the friends is service to the Kingdom of God."

The group had a long discussion about service. They all agreed they wanted to be of service to their community. Ruha asked the group, "If we want to serve the community, we need to know what service the community needs, right?"

"Right!"

"So, how can we know what the community needs?" Ruha continued.

"Ask them!" said one of the junior youth.

"So, shall we go ask our community what service would be helpful?"

"Yes!!"

Because the farms along the road between Kellyton and Choppy's Point were quite far apart, the group decided the best way to visit each family would be to drive. Rommy had left apples and muesli bars for everyone on the kitchen table. The junior youth picked them up on their way through the kitchen and out to the car.

When everyone had their seatbelts on, Ruha drove out of Fellowship Farm and turned right. When they came to the first farm, Ruha drove up the long driveway and parked out the front of the house. It was a large two-storey house. There was a car out the front. The junior youth climbed out of the van and went up to the front door. One of them knocked on the door. No one answered, but they could hear a dog barking inside the house. Another knocked more loudly. Still no one answered. "Should we knock again?" they asked Ruha.

"What do you think, would it be courteous to keep knocking?" The group agreed it would not be courteous. They climbed back into the van.

The next farm had a small wooden house, like the house at Fellowship Farm. The junior youth climbed out of the van again and rang the big metal bell that was hanging at the front. A woman came to the door. She was about 65 years old and she had a toothbrush and a hairbrush in her hand. She seemed a little surprised to see seven young people at her door, but she smiled and said, "Hello, how may I help you?"

Leezah and her friends suddenly realised that they had not thought about what they wanted to say. Leezah stepped forward.

"Hullo Mrs Henderson," she said.

"Hullo Leezah, what are you up to then?"

"Um, Mrs Henderson...my friends and I are part of a junior youth group."

"Oh, are you? That's nice. Is that like girl guides?"

"Well, a bit." Leezah didn't really know what the girl guides did. "We are participating in the Junior Youth Spiritual Empowerment Programme. And we want to be of service to the community. So we have come to ask if we can be of any service to you and Mr Henderson?"

"Oh!" Mrs Henderson made the sign of a cross in front of her heart. "Bless you Leezah! Surely the angels sent you." Mrs Henderson started to weep a little.

"What do you mean Mrs Henderson?" Leezah asked.

Mrs Henderson explained that her husband had had a heart attack the day before. He was being taken to a hospital in Melbourne for care, and might need surgery. Mrs Henderson was just in the middle of packing her things. She was going to the airport that night, to fly to Melbourne. But she didn't know what to do with her dog, Bernadette. The dog was old, but fit and healthy. She needed to be fed each day, and walked.

She asked the junior youth if they would care for her dog while she was away. The junior youth said they would. Mrs Henderson took each of them by the hand and thanked them with eyes full of gratitude. She then took them around to the back yard and introduced them to the dog.

Bernadette was a large, fat, friendly Labrador. Mrs Henderson showed them where the dog slept, in a basket on the patio outside the back door. She showed them where the bowls, the food, and the leash were kept. She gave Leezah her mobile phone number. Then she thanked them very much once again. The group left Mrs Henderson to her packing and climbed back into the van.

Inside the van, they started to consult. Only Leezah lived out on the same road as the

Hendersons' farm. The rest of the group lived in Kellyton. It would be impossible for them to get out to Mrs Henderson's house each day. But if only Leezah took care of the dog, it wasn't really a group service project.

"Maybe we could ask the school if we could keep the dog at school for the week? Then we could take it in turns to feed, walk, and clean up after Bernadette during lunch times," suggested one of the members.

"That's a great idea!" said another. Leezah agreed to take care of the dog on Sunday. And then on Monday they would talk with the principal about their junior youth group, the service project, and the idea to keep the dog at school. It seemed like a great idea.

The junior youth group visited a few more houses. One of the farmers asked the group to shear his sheep for him, but luckily he was only joking. The other families said they didn't need any service done, but they all said the group and the idea of service was a good one.

As Ruha drove the junior youth group back to Fellowship Farm, Leezah felt a great joy in her heart. It felt a bit like flying.

Bernadette gets stuck

On Sunday afternoon, when the family returned from shopping at the Kellyton market, Rommy drove Leezah, Skye-Maree and Olly to the Hendersons' property. Bernadette was happy to see them. She wagged her whole backside from side to side and dropped saliva from her panting tongue. The children gave her lots of cuddles. Then they collected her basket, bowls, leash and food and put them in the back of the Ute. Leezah had rung Mrs Henderson in Melbourne and asked if it was okay to bring Bernadette to Fellowship Farm. Mrs Henderson said it was a wonderful idea, as Bernadette would be so lonely on her own.

The puppies were already tied up on the back of the Ute. They were very excited to see Bernadette, and strained at their leashes trying to peer over the side of the tray. It was then that the family recognised their first problem. Bernadette was a big old dog. There was no way she could jump into the back of the Ute, the way the puppies did. She would also be very heavy and awkward to lift in, and her balance on the back of the moving Ute may not be very good.

"She could come in the cabin with us?" suggested Skye-Maree. Rommy nodded. Skye opened the back door of the Ute. Bernadette, with a bit of a gentle shove from the children, clambered in. The children clambered in after her.

When Rommy drove in to Fellowship Farm, she did not stop at the farm house. They had decided to take the dogs for a walk on the sand dunes behind the farm. Winter was a good time to walk on the dunes because it was hard work, and in summer it was very hot. Rommy drove up the hill paddock, through the apple orchard, down the side of the horse paddock to where the bush started. Then she parked the Ute.

Bernadette managed to clamber out of the Ute by herself. The children untied Flea, Flex, and Fizz from the back of the Ute. The puppies rushed to jump off and meet their new friend. At first Bernadette was overwhelmed by the excited puppies. She gave a yelp and nipped Flex on the bottom. Then the puppies ran off to explore the bush and left Bernadette in peace. Rommy and the children followed the trail through the bush toward the dunes. The puppies raced ahead, darting off to the side, crashing through the undergrowth, chasing lizards, each other, their tails, flies, and shadows. Bernadette followed at a good pace behind them, taking in the new smells.

Soon the bush became thinner, and the ground sandier. Instead of trees, there were just clumps of grass. Then the bush gave way to rolling hills of sand. The dunes rolled on and on for several kilometres until they reached the long beach that stretched all the way to Choppy's Point. The dunes ended at the same beach on which Leezah, Skye-Maree, Olly, Annissa and Nick had found the 'pirates'' buried bones when they were camping at the start of the year.

But today they would not walk all the way to the beach. They would just enjoy a run on the dunes close to the farm. The children ran up the first dune, slipping and sliding on the soft sand, with the puppies scrambling after them. Rommy and Bernadette came more slowly behind them. At the top of the dune the children could see more dunes ahead, going down and then up again. While they waited at the top of the dune for Rommy and Bernadette they looked for bits of wood that had turned white and crumbly. The pieces had the shape and feel of the original hard wood but crumbled to silky soft sand in their hands.

Rommy and Bernadette made it to the top of the sand dune. Bernadette was panting hard. Rommy gave her an encouraging pat. The puppies gathered around Bernadette again, sniffing and inviting her to play with them. "I think Bernadette and I had better wait here," said Rommy. "I'm worried she might get too tired if she tries to walk another dune. She might get stuck and not have the energy to return to the car!"

Normally when the Fitzgerald family ran on the sand dunes Rommy was one of the fastest and keenest. Skye-Maree knew it was a sacrifice for Rommy to sit with Bernadette instead of run on the dunes with the rest of them. She said, "I'll stay with Bernadette Mummy. You have a run on the dunes."

"That's kind and thoughtful Skye-Maree," said Rommy. "But I'll be fine here with Bernie." Skye-Maree gave her mother a hug. Then she yelled out, "Race you to the bottom. Last one there's a rotten egg."

The children and puppies charged off down the dune, while Olingah, who was leading the way, yelled out, "First one there has to eat it."

The flurry of activity caused excitement in Bernadette who picked herself up and lunged down the dune after the other dogs and children. Rommy jumped up after her but Bernadette was already running, sliding, rolling down the dune with the others. She let out barks of excitement and yelps of pain as her old body tumbled down the sandy mountain. Some seconds later, four sandy dogs and four sandy human beings arrived at the bottom, with grit in their hair, fur, eyes, ears and noses. Eight heads shook from side to side creating a shower of sand.

The dune ahead was even bigger than the one behind them. It towered before them like a yellow Everest reaching up to the clear blue winter sky. "Are you ready?" cried Leezah, "Let's go!" She started to scramble up the tower of sand. For every two meters she climbed, she slid back one meter. It was very slow going. The puppies were also struggling.

At the bottom, Bernadette was giving it a good Aussie go, but making very slow progress.

Very soon the winter jackets, hats and gloves felt way too hot. The children tucked their hats and gloves into the pockets of their jackets and left the jackets lying on the sand, halfway up the dune. They would collect them on the way back.

After twenty minutes of slippery struggle, the children and puppies arrived at the top of the sand dune, panting, thirsty, hot, sweaty, and sandy. Bernadette watched them from below where she had given up the struggle a while earlier. Rommy sat with Bernadette rubbing the neck, back and legs of the old dog. From the top of the dune the children could just see the sea, off in the hazy distance, past many kilometres of sand hills.

Suddenly, with a cry of "Ya-Bahá'u'l-Abhá" Skye-Maree threw herself back down the dune. Leaping, falling, rolling her way back toward her mother and Bernadette. Leezah and Olingah followed closely behind, grabbing their jackets as they tumbled down the hill. The puppies skidded, and slid, tumbled and bounded down the dune behind them, with sand in their ears, eyes and on their hot pink tongues.

When they arrived at the bottom, they were faced with the second challenge pertaining to Bernadette. This challenge was much greater than the challenge of getting her into the Ute. The family had to work out how they were going to get the fat old Labrador back up and over the sand dune to go home.

The first strategy they tried was encouragement. The Fitzgeralds went ahead of her up the slope and called her name, patting their legs, and encouraging her to follow. Bernadette did her best but her slow movements were no match for the quickly slipping sand.

The next strategy was to push her from behind. They hoped that if they helped her up the hill Bernadette would also put in an effort. But instead of putting in an effort, the dog dug her heels in and actively resisted the pushing. It was very uncomfortable for her to have four people pushing on her old bottom up a sandy hill, and she refused to go forward.

After some thought, the family decided to try a third strategy. They tied all the jackets together to make a kind of sled. Then they helped Bernadette onto her 'magic carpet'. Together the family pulled the dog up the sand hill. It was very hard work and only through their great unity and cooperation was it possible.

Just as they reached the top of the hill, there was a loud rip, and the sleeve of Olingah's jacket tore right off. But no-one was worried about Olingah's jacket at that point. They just wanted to make sure Bernadette didn't go sliding back down the hill. They all rushed to grab her and help her over the final peak of the dune.

When they had reached the top and made sure Bernadette was firmly planted on the correct side of the dune heading down toward the bush, the Ute, and the farm, the Fitzgeralds collapsed in a sweaty heap. Every muscle of every arm and leg ached.

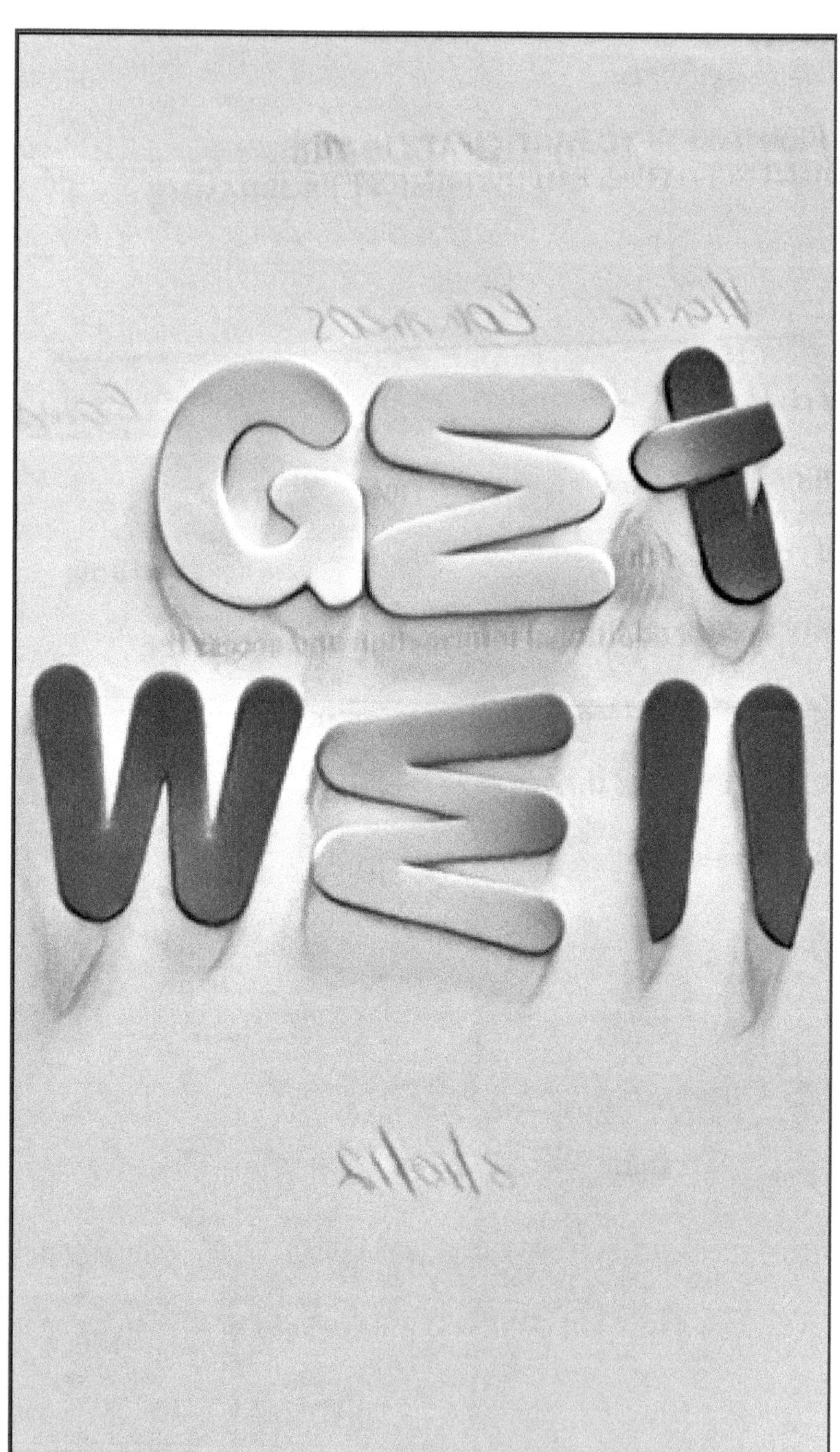

Get
Well

Prayers and preparation

When they arrived back at the farmhouse the number one priority was water! The dogs, the children, and Rommy felt like they were dying of thirst. Rommy tiptoed into the kitchen, trying not to drop sand, and grabbed some plastic cups. Back out in the garden the children filled the dogs' water bowls and watched them lap thirstily. They then filled the cups and did the same. After they had quenched their burning thirst, it was time to get clean. So that the sand would not be spread all the through the house, Rommy asked the children to take off all their clothes outside. The children stripped off their sandy layers until they were down to their underpants. When they had brushed as much sand as possible from their now freezing bodies, they ran through the house to Rommy and Flip's bathroom and jumped into the spa that was filling with warm soapy water.

After an hour in the warm bath, the bubbles had all burst, fingers had turned to prunes, and the bottom of the tub was covered with sand.

Leezah pulled out the plug and they wrapped themselves in the towels that Rommy had thoughtfully placed near the spa for them. When they had put on their pyjamas, dressing gowns and slippers, they went back to the spa and cleaned all the sand out of the bottom of the tub. Flip came in just as they were finishing. He was wearing an apron over his farm clothes. "Well, thank you for your cleanliness, thoughtfulness, and consideration! As a reward…there will be dinner this evening!"

"Daddy! We have dinner every evening!" said Skye-Maree.

"Well, I expect you can add gratitude to your list of virtues then," said Flip. "This is turning into a virtues festival!!"

"What's for dinner?" asked Leezah putting her hand over her father's mouth, "I am starving!"

"Vegetarian lasagne," replied Flip, when Leezah released her hand to let him speak. "Prepared by an extraordinarily beautiful chef and her extraordinarily handsome kitchen-hand. It is now ready to be served."

Olly, Leezah, Flip and Rommy set the table and served dinner, while Skye-Maree went to give the wallaby its evening feed. This would be the last evening feed of milk. From Monday the wallaby would only have one feed of milk per day, which would be in the mornings. In two weeks' time the family planned to take it to the back paddock, and encourage it to return to the bush. So it needed to be gradually weaned before then.

When Skye came back inside she was jumping from the cold, and raced to the fireplace to heat up before sitting down to dinner. She stood with her back to the fire and said, "Poor old Bernadette is fast asleep in her basket in the boot room. She didn't even stir when I went to get my boots."

"Bernadette the boot camp survivor!" said Flip, dishing the lasagne onto each of the plates.

"What's boot camp?" Skye asked, sitting down at the table.

"Boot camp is where you go camping wearing nothing but boots," replied Flip.

"In the rudey nudey?" asked Skye.

"But Bernadette didn't wear boots," said Olingah.

"True. True. Bernadette the paw camp survivor," said Flip.

"Let's say your prayer Skye and eat, before Mr. Goose Head here creates more confusion," Rommy pleaded.

"I wonder how the Hendersons are doing in Melbourne," Leezah wondered. "Imagine having a heart attack!"

"Yes, and going to hospital so far away!"

"And poor Mrs Henderson must be so worried. And she is far away from all her friends too."

"If we made them a card, could we send it to them at the hospital in Melbourne?" Leezah asked.

"Yes," said Rommy. "I think that is a splendid idea."

After dinner was eaten and the dishes were washed, Leezah, Skye-Maree, and Olingah sat back up at the dining table with coloured cardboard, felt pens, glitter, and glue, to make cards for Mr and Mrs Henderson. They decided to put one line from the healing prayer in each card. So Leezah wrote: "Thy Name is my healing, O my God, and remembrance of Thee is my remedy …" Skye wrote, "Nearness to Thee is my hope, and love for Thee is my companion." Olingah wrote, "Thy mercy to me is my healing and my succour in both this world and the world to come."

In the middle of making the cards the phone rang. Flip was in the kitchen making the school lunches for the next day so he answered the phone, but with an English accent: "Good evening. Fitzgerald residence. How may I be of assistance?"

Flip leaned through the doorway of the kitchen and said, "Miss Fitzgerald senior, a phone call for you."

The children hardly ever received phone calls. Leezah jumped up and ran to the phone.

It was Ruha.

"Hi Leezah!" said Ruha joyfully.

"Hi Ruha!!" said Leezah.

"How was day one of the service project?"

"Oh it was great, except we nearly killed Bernadette!"

"Oh!" exclaimed Ruha, laughing. "Tell me more!" Leezah started to giggle. She told Ruha about Bernadette's boot camp.

Ruha asked her if she was feeling ready to talk to the principal of Kellyton Primary about the Junior Youth Spiritual Empowerment Programme, and their service project. Leezah felt her heart beat faster. She had forgotten about that.

Ruha helped her think about what she might need to take from the Bahá'í Supplies cupboard. She also helped her think about how to talk to the principal about the service project. When the phone call finished, Leezah felt confident about talking to the principal.

"Thanks Ruha," she said, "It's been very helpful talking to you."

"You're welcome cherub."

Leezah went to the Bahá'í Supplies cupboard and took some pamphlets on the Junior Youth Spiritual Empowerment Programme and put it in her school bag. Tomorrow she would give one to the principal.

When Leezah came back to the table to finish her card, she saw that Olingah and Skye-Maree had finished theirs already. "Want some help sister?" asked Olly.

"Yes, please!" said Leezah. "Let's stick the glitter on together."

Together they quickly finished the cards and put away the art supplies. The children left the cards on the table so the glue could dry. Rommy promised to take them to the post office the next day.

As Flip examined their work he exclaimed, "Captivating creativity! Edifying excellence! And unassailable unity! Bravo! Bravo!"

Before the family had their evening prayers, Leezah asked them to pray that she would do a good job talking to the principal the next day.

"We shall pray for you to be a pure channel darling," promised Rommy. Flip reached for the guitar and started to play: "O God! Make me a hollow reed, from which the pith of self hath been blown, that I may become a pure channel, through which Thy love may flow unto others."

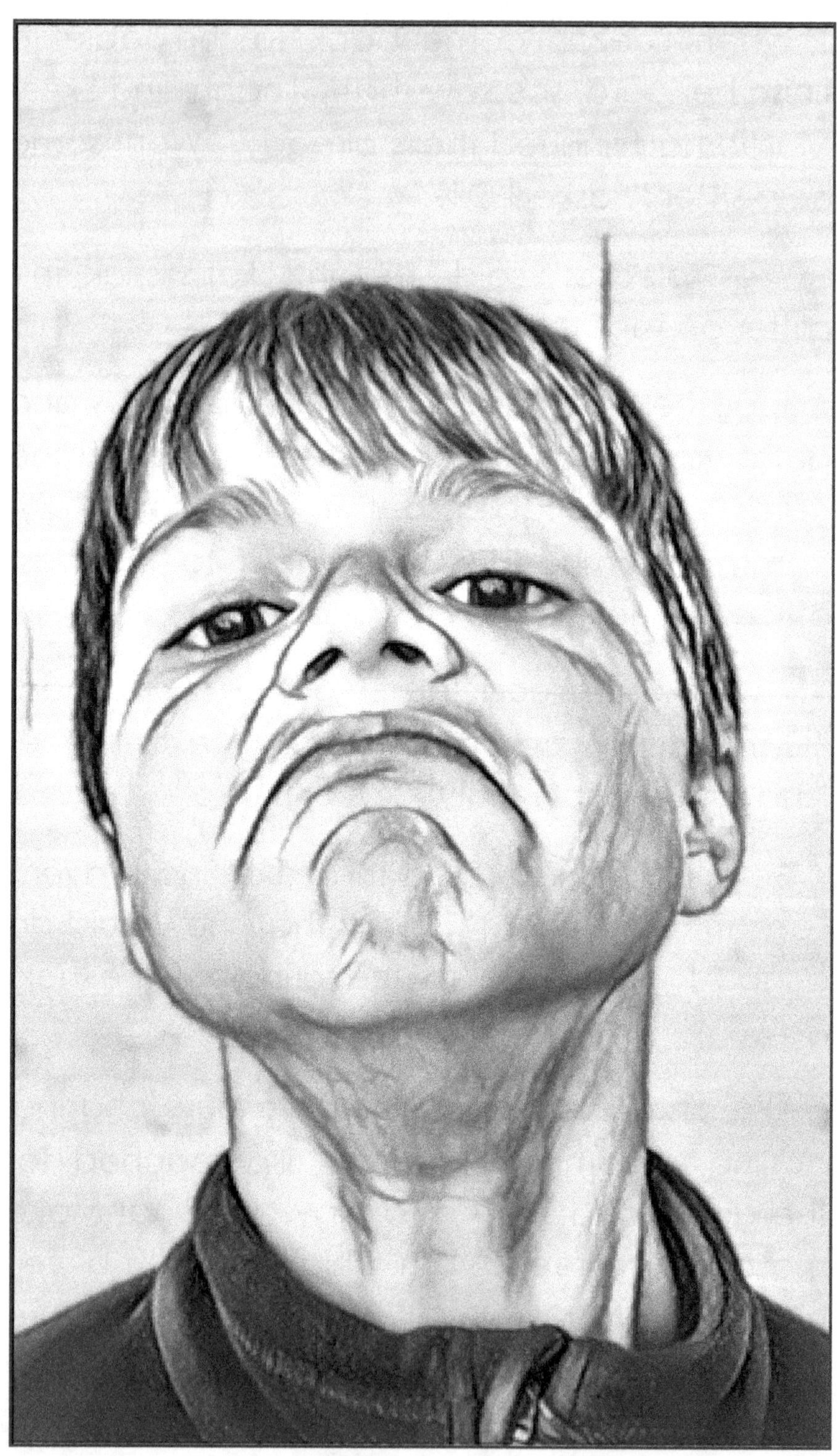

Qualms and courage

A light rain was falling as Leezah, Skye-Maree and Olingah said goodbye to Flea, Flex, Fizz, Bernadette, and Joey. They went to wait for the school bus. When it arrived, at 7:30, they climbed on, greeting the bus driver: "Good morning Ms Rowbottom."

"Look at your dirty shoes making a mess of my bus!" grumbled Ms Rowbottom. She pulled the door shut with the leaver next to her seat. The children chose their seats near the middle of the bus. They were the first to be picked up, so they could sit anywhere.

As the bus stopped at farms along the way to Kellyton, their schoolmates joined them and soon the bus was full of chattering children, sharing news of their weekend. One of the younger boys sat across the aisle from Leezah and Skye, reading a book. A boy from Leezah's class, Wayne, leaned over from the seat behind and grabbed the book, knocking the younger boy in the head as he did so. Wayne pretended to read the book out loud, making up the words, using a squeaky voice.

Then he threw the book to his friend at the back of the bus. The younger boy didn't turn around. He focused his attention out the window and pulled his knees up to his chest. Leezah could see he was afraid of the big year six student. Skye-Maree stood up from her seat and faced the back of the bus. "Give it back Wayne," she said courageously.

"Make me," said Wayne, sticking out his tongue.

The book was being thrown about the back of the bus.

Skye stood up and walked to the back of the bus, holding on to the seats so she wouldn't fall over as Ms Rowbottom dodged the potholes. As the book flew through the air Skye-Maree reached out to grab it. She missed and fell on top of the boy who had thrown it. He pushed her and she fell on the floor of the bus. Suddenly Ms Rowbottom slammed on the brakes of the bus. Skye slid on the floor, collecting mud and gravel on her clean school uniform.

"Skye-Maree Fitzgerald! Wayne Jones! Up the front! Now!" she hollered.

Skye-Maree stood up and tried to wipe off the mud that was smeared all down the back of her pants, as she walked down the aisle. Wayne followed after her.

"Sit!" barked Ms Rowbottom, pointing to the two empty seats at the front of the bus.

When the two children were seated, the bus continued its journey toward Kellyton Primary. Leezah picked up the book from where it had fallen on the floor of the bus, and gave it back to the boy who had been reading it.

Leezah then snuck down to the front of the bus, hoping Ms Rowbottom wouldn't see her and get cross. The other children watched her and thought she was going to comfort Skye-Maree. But when she got to the front of the bus she sat herself in the seat next to Wayne. Wayne was surprised to see Leezah, and even more surprised to see she was smiling at him.

"Hey Wayne," she said.

"Hey," Wayne replied.

"What did you do on the weekend?" Wayne was expecting Leezah to have a go at him about what he had done. He felt confused.

"Nothing," he answered. Then he added, "Watched t.v.."

"Boring?" asked Leezah.

"Yep."

"We had junior youth group at my place this weekend," Leezah said.

"What's that?" Wayne asked.

Leezah told Wayne about the group and about the service project they were working on that week. She invited him to join the group.

Wayne asked, "Is it all girls?"

Leezah nodded.

"Yuuuk!" said Wayne.

"But the programme is for boys and girls. If you joined the group, you could invite some of your friends too. It's great if there are boys and girls in the group."

Leezah had some flyers about the programme in her bag to give to the principal. Just as the bus pulled up at the school, she pulled one out and gave it to Wayne. Wayne shoved it in his bag, and jumped off the bus.

Leezah went with Skye-Maree to see if there was a pair of pants in lost property that she could borrow for the day, as her pants were covered in mud. Mr Springbett was in charge of lost property and first aid. He was in his office when they arrived. "Hullo Leezah. Hullo Skye-Maree," he said. "Have you been rolling in the mud?"

Mr Springbett had two pairs of navy blue uniform pants in lost property. One was very tight and one was too long. Skye chose the long pants and rolled them up. She put her muddy pants in a plastic bag that Mr Springbett gave her. The sisters thanked Mr Springbett and went to class.

As it got closer to recess, Leezah found it harder and harder to concentrate. At recess she was going to talk to the principal about the junior youth programme. She was also going to ask if Bernadette could stay at the school for the week. She wondered what the principal would say. Leezah hoped she wouldn't forget what she wanted to say to the principal. By the time the bell rang for the end of class, Leezah was feeling so nervous she jumped at the sound of the bell and nearly fell off her chair.

The girls in the junior youth group gathered outside the year six classroom. They walked together to the principal's office. To get to the principal's office they had to go through the office of her secretary. As they walked in, Leezah saw Wayne sitting on the couch, waiting for the principal. "Girls?" said the secretary, looking up from his computer, "What are you after?"

Leezah swallowed anxiously. The other girls, on either side of her, squeezed her hands. "Um, we'd like to see Ms Vermeer, please."

"What about?"

"About a service project we're doing, and about the junior youth programme," said Leezah timidly.

"Well, Ms Vermeer is on the phone at the moment, and then she will need to see Wayne. But if you'd like to wait, she may have time to see you before the end of recess." The girls nodded, and sat down on the long couch against the wall, next to Wayne.

Just as they sat down, they heard Ms Vermeer hang up the phone. Her door opened and she came into the waiting area.

"Hullo Wayne. Hullo girls," she said as the children stood up to greet their principal. "Are you all together?"

"Yes!" said Leeza, surprising herself.

"Actually, no!" said the secretary, thinking that Leezah was trying to push in, and see the principal without waiting.

Before she had time to think, Leezah said, "Ms Vermeer, maybe if you see us all together, you won't need to see Wayne afterward." Everyone looked puzzled, especially Wayne. But Ms Vermeer nodded and welcomed the children into her office.

In Ms Vermeer's office there were only three chairs, but there were five children, so they all stood.

"How can I help?" asked Ms Vermeer, seated behind her desk.

Everyone looked at Leezah.

Leezah said a prayer in her head: "Yá Bahá'u'l-Abhá! Yá Bahá'u'l-Abhá!" She prayed that `Abdul'-Bahá would be with her. And then she began to speak.

Leezah told the principal about the junior youth programme and gave her the flyer. She also told her about Mr Henderson's heart attack and the group's service project. She asked if Bernadette could stay at the school for a week so the members of the group could share the work of caring for her.

Then Leezah said that she had invited Wayne to join the group. Leezah suggested that instead of giving Wayne detention for his bullying on the bus, maybe Ms Vermeer might let him off, if he agreed to try the junior youth programme.

Ms Vermeer listened carefully to all that Leezah said. Then she said:

"Thank you for telling me about this Leezah. This sounds like a wonderful programme and a very important service project. I think we can find a place for Bernadette in the fenced area next to the kindergarten. I will talk to Mr Springbett about setting up a space for her. As you suggest Leezah, your group can spend recess, lunch and some time after school feeding, walking, and cleaning up after Bernadette. If Wayne would like to try the programme, I am more than happy for him to do that instead of detention. And I think we should tell all the year sixes about this programme. Would you girls be happy to talk about it to your class?"

Leezah felt a wave of relief and joy flood over her. Inside her head she said again Yá Bahá'u'l-Abhá. The other girls looked nervous about talking in front of the class, but Leezah said, "Yes, we would love to." Ms Vermeer turned to Wayne and said, "Wayne, would you like to try the junior youth programme, or would you like to stay and have a 'chat' with me?"

"The programme," said Wayne without hesitation. He had had quite a few 'chats' with the principal this year and he didn't want to have any more.

Quest for a cruise

The children left the principal's office just before the bell for the end of recess rang. Leezah hurried to the front office to call her mother.

"How did it go?" asked Rommy, when she answered the phone.

"It was GREAT!" said Leezah loudly. The office staff looked up from their computers and scowled. "I will tell you everything tonight," Leezah continued more quietly. "But could you please bring Bernadette to the school when you come in to work this afternoon? Ms Vermeer said she can stay for the week."

"Well done courageous girl!" said Rommy with delight. "I will bring her to the school at lunch time. See you then my darling!"

Leezah hung up the phone, thanked the office staff, and went outside to join Wayne and the other junior youth. The bell rang, and they walked back to the year six classroom together. Before class started, Leezah got

Wayne's home phone number so Ruha could talk to Wayne's parents about the junior youth programme.

Once again, it was hard for Leezah to concentrate on her work, but this time it wasn't because she was nervous. It was because she was bursting with joy. She had practiced courage and determination, drawing on prayer and trust in God, and the junior youth group had experienced immediate confirmation!

At lunch time, Rommy pulled in to the school in the orange Ute. Leezah and the junior youth were waiting for her under the oak tree. When Rommy opened the door and Bernadette lumbered out, she was immediately surrounded by children. Rommy clipped the leash on to Bernadette's collar. Everyone wanted to be the one to hold the leash while Bernadette walked to her new temporary home.

Leezah suggested Wayne be the one to hold the leash. The other three members of the group thought that was a very unfair idea. In the end, the three girls in the junior youth group, other than Leezah, all held the leash together.

Many children gathered around to find out what was going on. They helped Wayne, Leezah and Rommy to carry the dog bed, bowls, food, brush, and doggy-do bags from the car to the fenced area near the kindergarten. They filled the bowls with food and water, and placed Bernadette's basket under the roof of the open shed.

Bernadette was having a lovely time, being patted and fussed over. She was very happy to have some extra food in the middle of the day. She then wandered around the grassy area sniffing the new smells. She was followed by a large group of excited children who were taking it in turns to brush her.

The junior youth thought it would be good to make up a roster to care for Bernadette. She would need food and water each day. She would need to be walked. She would need to have her poo cleaned up, and her fur brushed. Some of the members of the group didn't have to catch the school bus home after school, so they promised to care for her after school. Leezah and Wayne promised to care for her at recess and lunch, and they all agreed to check on her before school.

When the bell for the end of lunch rang, Rommy hugged Leezah, and said goodbye to the other students. As Rommy drove off to the veterinary clinic, many arms waved her goodbye. The students went to their classrooms to finish their school day.

In her classes after lunch Leezah again had trouble concentrating. This time it was because she was thinking about Ms Vermeer's request for Leezah to talk to the whole year six class about the junior youth programme and the service project. She had an idea, and once it got into her head, Leezah couldn't get it out.

Leezah wanted to take photos of her junior youth group and make a PowerPoint presentation. She would photograph them with their animator, Ruha; doing their study; doing their art activities; and playing their games. Then she would take photos of Bernadette and the service project and she would put it together with some captions and music to present to her class.

On the bus on the way home, Leezah told Skye-Maree about what Ms Vermeer had said, and about her idea. "The only problem is we don't have a camera," said Skye.

"Why do you want a camera for?" asked Wayne who was sitting behind them and had caught the last part of their conversation. Leezah turned to face him. She explained the idea she had for presenting the programme to the class.

"I have a camera," said Wayne, tossing a dirty tennis ball in the air and catching it. "I got it from my grandmother for Christmas. It's digital."

Leezah wasn't sure if Wayne was offering his camera or bragging.

"We could use that to take the photos," he added. Leezah grinned.

"Thanks Wayne!" Wayne agreed to bring the camera to school the next day to take photos of Bernadette and the junior youth.

That evening, after the children had finished their chores, Leezah shared the exciting events of the day with the rest of the family. The family was making vegetable soup for dinner, with fruit salad for dessert. As it was the middle of winter, it was expensive to buy fresh fruit. Flip passed Leezah a can of pineapples to open. Before she opened the can, Leezah read the label. Next to the picture of pineapple slices was a picture of a large boat. Leezah read that by sending in two labels from the pineapple cans she could enter into a competition to go on a family cruise. Leezah checked the cupboard to see if there were any more tins of pineapple. She found three more.

"Daddy, may we enter into this competition?" asked Leezah. "If we win, we get to go on a cruise."

"Like my friend Laurie!" said Skye-Maree.

"Of course we can enter," replied Flip. "First we need to make dinner. Then you can take the labels off the cans and fill them out."

"Thanks Daddy," said Leezah.

After dinner Leezah called Ruha. She told her all about the conversation with the principal, and gave her Wayne's mother's phone number. A few minutes later Ruha called Leezah back, to say Wayne's mother said he could come to the group if he wants to. Ruha told them she would pick him up on the way through to Fellowship Farm in two weeks' time.

While Skye and Olingah read by the fire, Leezah cut the labels off the pineapple cans. Using a permanent pen she wrote

Pineapples In Juice

on the silver cans, so that they would remember what was in them. Then she filled in the questions on the inside of the labels. The first questions were easy – name, address, phone number. Then Leezah had to say in 20 words or less why they wanted to go on the cruise.

"Why do we want to go on the cruise?" she asked her family. "We only have 20 words to answer the question."

The Fitzgeralds realised they didn't really have any idea what a cruise would be like. The label of the pineapple can said the boat would go to many different countries in the Pacific Ocean. In the end Leezah wrote: "We want to unite the world so it would be good to visit our brothers and sisters in other countries." It was exactly 20 words.

She put the labels in an envelope and addressed it according to the instructions. She added a stamp from the stationery cupboard. She asked Rommy to post it the next day. Rommy said she would.

There was still an hour until Leezah's bedtime, when she sat down to have her hair plaited for bed. After her busy day, Leezah was exhausted. The family sang their evening prayers with much joy. To everyone's surprise, Leezah then kissed her parents good night and went off to bed at the same time as Olingah.

Lying in bed she reflected on her day. She was glad she had invited Wayne to the junior youth group. She was thankful that Mr Springbett had some clean pants for Skye-Maree. She was grateful for `Abdul'-Bahá's help at the principal's office. She was very happy that the principal had agreed to have Bernadette at the school. She was relieved that Wayne's mother had agreed to Wayne joining the junior youth group.

She hoped Wayne would also invite some of his friends. And she also hoped that the entries into the competition from the pineapple cans would win them a trip on a big boat! That was Leezah's final thought, as she quickly drifted off to sleep.

Giving is getting

When the children woke the following morning the air in the bedroom was very cold. They could hear pouring rain pelting against the windows and roof of the farmhouse. After prayers and breakfast, the children dressed in their warmest clothes, raincoats, rain hats and gumboots, and piled into the Ute. Flip drove them around the farm in the dark and rain, so they could attend to their morning chores without getting drenched.

They took it in turns to jump out of the Ute at the pig sty, the shed where the working dogs were tied up, and the hen house. And when they got back to the farm house Olingah fed the wallaby some milk, while Skye-Maree fed the puppies and Leezah fed the pigeons. When they finished their morning service, they shook the water from their rain coats and boots, and left them hanging in the boot room.

When they arrived at school at 8:10, it was still raining. Olingah and Skye-Maree hurried off to their classrooms. Leezah and Wayne went from the bus to Bernadette. The other junior youth were already there, sheltered under the shed roof. In the rain, the service project didn't seem like so much fun. Bernadette's wet fur stank, so no one wanted to brush her. There were two poos on the cement floor of the shed to clean up. Taking Bernadette for a walk in the cold rain was very uninviting. And her food bowl was full of ants.

Reluctantly the junior youth began to attend to the tasks. As soon as they had finished, they rushed off to the toilets to wash their hands, and hurried to their warm classrooms.

Wayne had brought the camera, and Leezah took some photos of Bernadette and the junior youth. But the sky was dark grey, so the photos were dark, and the junior youth did not seem very joyful as they served. At recess time, Leezah went to check on Bernadette, but Wayne was nowhere to be seen. Bernadette sat in her basket, with her head between her paws. Leezah didn't want to smell like wet dog for the rest of the day, but she felt sorry for Bernadette. She gave her a rub down with the brush until just before the bell. Because she was with Bernadette, Leezah didn't have time to eat her recess snacks.

During her classes between recess and lunch Leezah's tummy growled with hunger.

By lunch time, the rain had stopped. The air was still cold, and the grass was soggy. Bernadette still smelt like a mixture of mouldy old carpet and a swamp. The junior youth checked on her quickly. They complained about the cold, and after a few minutes they hurried back to their classroom. "I hope the Hendersons come home soon," said one of the girls. "I'm sick of taking care of Bernadette." It had been less than one day!

"Me too," another agreed.

"Me three."

The junior youth took care of Bernadette for the rest of the week. Sometimes it was fun, and there were fights over who took her for a walk around the school ground. Sometimes it was not fun, and dog poo had to be cleaned off shoes and fingers. The junior youth complained about Bernadette some days, and smothered her in cuddles on other days. Leezah took photos of everything.

On Friday morning Mrs Henderson called Rommy to say she and Mr Henderson would be returning to the farm that afternoon. Rommy sent a message to Leezah, Skye and Olly through the school office. She told them to wait at school and not catch the bus. After she had finished her work, Rommy came to the school in the Ute and collected the children, Bernadette, and Bernadette's belongings. They stopped at the Hendersons' farm on the way home to return the dog to her home. They settled Bernadette back into her regular place on the back porch, and filled her bowls with food and water.

Just as they were getting back into the Ute, the Hendersons arrived from the airport. Mr Henderson looked pale and frail. Mrs Henderson and Rommy helped him into the house. When he was settled in a comfortable chair, Mrs Henderson came back outside, and turned her attention to the children.

"Thank you for your beautiful cards," she said. "We received them yesterday." The children smiled. Then Mrs Henderson turned her attention to Leezah.

"How was Bernadette?" she asked with tears in her eyes. "We were so grateful to know she was being cared for by your girl guides group."

Leezah remembered all the times the group had complained and grumbled about taking care of Bernadette. She remembered the times the junior youth had rushed their service and hurried to get back to the warm classroom. She felt embarrassed by Mrs Henderson's gratitude, and unworthy of the praise.

"It was our pleasure," said Leezah. "Thank you for trusting us with Bernadette."

Mrs Henderson reached into the back of her car. She pulled out a bag with four little presents, carefully wrapped. (Mrs Henderson didn't know there was a new fifth member of the group.) Leezah realised that even though it was a very difficult time for Mrs Henderson in Melbourne, she had taken time to get thank you gifts for the junior youth.

Leezah felt very embarrassed. "Thank you very much Mrs Henderson," she said, accepting the bag of gifts. Skye-Maree and Olingah were very curious to know what was inside the boxes wrapped in purple paper, tied with white ribbon.

"No, no, no, thank you my dear. Please convey our gratitude to the members of your group."

"I will," promised Leezah.

When the Fitzgeralds were in the Ute and on their way home, Olingah said: "Open the present Leezah! Open the present!"

Leezah shook her head. Olingah pleaded: "Can I then? Pleeease? Can I open it for you?"

"No Olly," said Leezah.

"Why not??" said Olingah. "Aren't you busting to see what it is?"

Leezah nodded. "I want to see what's inside too. But Mrs Henderson didn't know we now have five members of our group. So I need to give my present to Wayne. He helped nearly every day."

"I honour your sacrifice Leezah," said Rommy quietly, smiling as she drove.

"Oh no, I don't!" said Olingah. "It might be yummy chocolates!" But Olingah wasn't really upset, just curious. In fact, he really admired how strong and selfless his sister was. "Can I just have a little peak and then wrap it again?"

Leezah laughed. She knew what the wrapping would look like after Olly's little peak. "No Olly. You'll have to wait 'til we catch the bus on Monday and Wayne opens his present."

Wayne was known on the bus for being a bit of a bully. So it was unusual for him to be greeted warmly on the bus, especially by younger children. Everyone was usually a bit scared of him. He was very surprised when he got on the bus on Monday morning to find Olingah waiting for him at the very front seat. Olingah had a big smile on his face and a small purple gift in his hand. "This is for you!" he exclaimed, thrusting the gift at Wayne.

"What for?" asked Wayne walking toward the back of the bus, followed by Olingah, as Ms Rowbottom shut the bus door.

"It's from Mrs Henderson. To say thank you for taking care of Bernadette. Do you want to open it?" asked Olingah. Wayne swung into a seat near the back of the bus. Olingah climbed in after him.

"Sure," said Wayne, dropping his school bag on the floor.

"What do you think it is?" asked Olingah excitedly.

"Dunno," replied Wayne. "Maybe a pony."

Wayne started to open the gift, but as he did so, he realised how excited Olingah was about it. He tossed the gift to Olingah. "Why don't you open it?"

"Thanks Wayne!" exclaimed Olingah. Wayne half smiled, half smirked at Olingah, but inside he was feeling something he hadn't felt before. It felt good.

Olingah opened the gift. Inside was a box of chocolate covered toffees.

"Oh look! Toffees!" exclaimed Olingah. "Here you go Wayne." Olingah reluctantly passed the box and wrapping paper to Wayne.

"You can have them Olingah," said Wayne, surprising even himself. As soon as he said those words he felt a burst of happiness in his heart. And so did Olingah!

Goodbye Joey

Every morning for the rest of the week Olingah went to have a chat with the wallaby in the front 'garden'. The wallaby was no longer given milk, just a few pellets. It snuffled around Olingah's waist searching for the bottle. Olingah explained over and over again that he didn't have any milk, but the wallaby kept searching. Olingah was not looking forward to releasing the wallaby into the bush on the weekend.

Saturday arrived. Olingah woke with a heavy heart and Leezah woke with a joyful heart. Two things were happening. Ruha, and the other animators, the junior youth, and Wayne were coming to Fellowship Farm for the junior youth group. At the same time, the Fitzgeralds, along with the junior youth group, were taking the wallaby to the bush to release it into the wild.

As usual when Ruha arrived with her van full of youth and junior youth, Leezah, Skye-Maree and Olingah were waiting at the front gate to greet them. Ruha greeted each of them with an enormous smile and a bear hug. She looked into their faces and could immediately see that Olingah was not happy. "My love, my love, why are you sad today?" she said to him, giving him an extra hug.

The sadness in his heart and the loving kindness burning in Ruha's heart mixed together, and Olingah started to weep. As the other youth and junior youth piled out of the van and headed inside, Ruha scooped Olly up in her strong brown arms and carried him into the house. He told Ruha about the plans to release the wallaby. He told her how very sad he felt about it. Ruha's tender heart couldn't bear to see Olly suffering. She started to weep with Olly and soon both of them were sitting in the sunroom crying.

After a few minutes, the rest of the group was settled and ready to start. Rommy appeared at the doorway. Olly and Skye reluctantly left the room with their mother. Ruha took a tissue from her sleeve and blew her nose. Her eyes were red, but she was smiling.

"Firstly a very warm welcome to our new member, Wayne, who has already participated in a service project!" The group clapped to welcome Wayne. Leezah snapped her first photos of the junior youth group in session and continued to quietly take photos for the rest of the session.

"To help Wayne understand more about the junior youth programme we are going to do an activity that some of us have done before,' said Ruha, after prayers.

Ruha took out a round plastic container of dirt from her bag. She took the lid off, and asked the group what they could see. Everyone said they could just see a bowl of dirt. Ruha especially asked Wayne. Wayne said he could see dirt and small rocks. Ruha smiled and said, "Well done. That's right."

Then she passed the bowl to Wayne and asked him to see what he could find. Wayne stuck his fingers into the dirt and dug around. Soon he came across a glass gem, and then another, and another. Ruha passed the bowl to the other junior youth and they also found glass gems under the dirt.

Ruha said: "So when we looked at this bowl we thought there was just dirt in it, didn't we? But underneath the dirt we found gems.

People can be like that. Sometimes we look at each other and we don't much like what we see. But underneath the dirt, in every single one of us, are hundreds of gems." Ruha gave everyone a page with some words on it. "Wayne, could you please read this for us?"

Wayne read: "Regard man as a mine rich in gems of inestimamam inestimama inestimable value."

"Well done!" said Ruha, smiling and nodding. "We are like mines rich in gems of great value! What do you think Wayne, if we cut us open would we find gold and silver inside of us?"

"No, derr," said Wayne.

"So what are the gems inside of us?"

Wayne wasn't sure how to answer, so the other junior youth helped him.

"They are the virtues."

"Like kindness and courage."

"Helpfulness."

"Assertiveness."

"Obedience."

"Yes!" exclaimed Ruha. "And are these gems in all of us, or only in some of us?"

"All of us!" replied the junior youth.

"But sometimes they are hidden deep down under the dirt," said Leezah, and everyone laughed.

"True!" said Ruha.

Next Ruha explained that after their next chapter of Breezes of Confirmation the junior youth group was going to participate in releasing the wallaby into the bush. "What virtues or gems will we need to practice when we do that?" she asked, her eyes sparkling with love.

"We will need gentleness and patience," said Leezah, so the wallaby can slowly adjust to its new surroundings.

"We will need compassion, to support Olingah," said one of the junior youth, remembering Olingah's tears.

"And we'll need trust, to let the wallaby go into the bush when we want to keep it here where we know it is safe."

"Good one!" said Ruha. "And if Rommy gives us instructions we need to follow them. What's that called Wayne?"

Wayne wasn't really sure. Wayne felt like he was learning a new language.

"That's okay," said Ruha as she saw Wayne wasn't sure. "It's called obedience." Wayne nodded.

Ruha handed out the copies of Breezes of Confirmation, including a brand new copy for Wayne, with his name on the front. Ruha asked the junior youth to fill Wayne in on the story and concepts so far. Then they continued their study together.

After the study, the group left the sunroom and joined Rommy, Flip, Olingah and Skye-Maree in the living room. From there, everyone went outside to put on their coats, hats, gloves and boots. In single file they walked around to the front of the house, taking care not to let the puppies out of the back garden.

Out the front of the house was the orange Ute. The back of the tray was open. The youth and junior youth climbed in, along with Olingah and Skye-Maree. Rommy opened the cabin of the Ute for Flip. He picked up the wallaby from the front garden, and holding it firmly, he climbed into the back of the Ute cabin. Rommy closed the tray and encouraged the young people to hold on tightly.

Rommy drove through the gate into the hill paddock behind the farm house. She continued through the apple orchard and over to the back of the property where the bush started. When she had parked the Ute under a big old gum tree, the youth climbed off the back, slowly and quietly. Rommy opened the door of the cabin for Flip, who climbed out. Flip put the wallaby on the grass.

At first the wallaby seemed confused. Then it spotted Olingah and lolloped over to him. The wallaby started to snuffle around Olingah's waist, hoping for a treat. Olingah rubbed his hands through the wallaby's soft fur, and started to cry again. "Off you go little fella," he said quietly. "Off you go home."

After some time, it was clear the wallaby was not going to head for the bush while its friends were there. Rommy suggested they head back to the farm house. Olingah gave

the wallaby one last goodbye stroke. With
tears streaming down his face, he climbed into
the back of the Ute. The others gathered
around him and embraced him in a big group
hug all the way back down to the farm house.

Hullo again Joey!

Back at the farmhouse the junior youth group continued its session. It was preparing the presentation for the year six class. Some of the photographs Leezah had taken were blurry, some were too close, some too far away, but some were okay. The junior youth chose the best photos to use in the PowerPoint presentation for the class. Ruha helped them to get the photos off the camera and onto her laptop, and showed them how to use PowerPoint to make a presentation.

The group included photos of the good times: digging in the dirt for gems, joyfully walking Bernadette around the school; opening their presents from Mrs Henderson. And they chose photos that showed challenges: cleaning dog poo off their shoe; crying as the wallaby was released; walking Bernadette in the cold rain. They chose captions for the photos, and music to go with their presentation. At first nobody but Leezah had the courage to talk in front of the class. After Ruha lead some discussion about confirmation, however, they all agreed to try and help with the presentation. Wayne said he would like to do the digging in the dirt for gems activity with the class. He would then talk about the virtues. The others thought this was a great idea.

The junior youth made bookmarks with the quote 'Regard man as a mine rich in gems of inestimable value' on them, to give to the teacher and all the students. Ruha gave them registration forms which the students could take home to their parents to fill out, if they wanted to join a junior youth group. By the time the junior youth group finished its session, the junior youth were excited about presenting to their class on Monday.

The group finished with a prayer and a snack before heading out to the van. Olingah, Skye and Leezah stood at the gate of Fellowship Farm and waved to their friends until the van was completely out of sight. As they walked back to the house, the yard felt empty with no friends, no Joey, and no Bernadette. The sun was already sinking in the sky and the air was icy.

The children went inside. Flip had just added some logs to the fire in the living room. The children consulted about whether to play Monopoly or Chinese Checkers. After a few rounds of scissors paper rock, they agreed on Chinese Checkers. They sat on the rug by the fire, moving the coloured marbles until Skye-Maree had all her marbles in the triangle opposite her starting place. Just as they packed up, Flip came in to the living room from the kitchen and said, "How about some home-made vegetarian pizza for dinner?"

"YUM!" the three of them agreed.

Out in the kitchen Rommy put some music on. While they sang along to the barnyard boogey, the family grated cheese, and chopped onions, capsicum, mushrooms, pineapple, olives, and sun-dried tomatoes. They covered their pizza bases with tomato paste and toppings and slipped them into the oven to bake.

Twenty minutes later, the family was gathered around the dining table. Plates were covered in generously topped pizzas. Long strings of melted cheese stretched from plates to hungry mouths. Faces and fingers were covered in tomato paste and other toppings.

"I am so glad that no animals died to make this pizza," said Olingah suddenly. "I hope we never ever eat meat again."

"I agree," said Leezah.

"Let's make a toast," said Flip.

"Toast?" asked Olingah.

"A toast," said Flip. "Hold up your glasses."

Everyone held up their glasses, with their greasy fingers.

"I hereby declare the Fitzgerald home to be vegetarian," Flip announced.

"Hear hear," cried Rommy

"Hear hear," the children copied their mother.

The family clinked glasses and drank their juice.

After dinner, the family sat by the fire to read and play cards. After a few minutes Flip went to the kitchen and pulled a bag out of the pantry cupboard. It was full of something he had bought with Rommy at the Kellyton markets that morning. He took the bag over to the fire place.

"What's in there?" asked Skye.

"I'll act it out for you and if you guess it correctly, we can all eat them."

"Charades!' cried Leezah.

Olingah was more excited about what there might be to eat in the bag.

Flip held up one finger.

"One word," said Rommy.

Flip put his finger to his nose, which meant, "correct".

Then he put two fingers of one hand against the opposite arm.

"Two syllables," said Leezah.

Flip again touched the side of his nose.

Then he put one finger against the opposite arm.

"First syllable," said Skye.

Flip nodded and pointed to his shirt.

"Chocolate!" cried Olingah, not because he thought that was the clue, but because he hoped that was what was in the bag.

Flip shook his head vigorously, and pointed again to the top half of his body.

"Marshmallows!" cried Olingah.

Flip silently lifted Olingah onto the couch and tickled him, before resuming.

"Shirt?" "Jumper?" "Top?" "Chest?"

Flip banged his nose so vigorously that Olingah thought Flip would get a blood nose.

"First syllable, chest," said Skye.

Then Flip put two fingers against the opposite arm.

"Second syllable," called Rommy.

Flip acted out holding something small, breaking it open, and eating the insides.

"Nut!" cried Leezah.

Again Flip hit his nose so much with his hand that he seemed at risk of breaking it.

"Chestnut" cried Skye.

"Bravo!" cried Flip.

Inside the bag were shiny brown chestnuts. The children put them on the little shovel beside the fire place and pushed them into the coals at the side of the fire. They left them there while they played cards and read.

After about 15 minutes there were some popping sounds coming from the fire. The children pulled the little shovel out and Flip tested the nuts. Together Rommy and Flip pulled the hot outer shell off the chestnuts leaving the soft warm nut exposed. The children ate the hot sweet creamy nuts, while the next batch roasted in the fire. It was the perfect evening snack for a cold winter night.

When the chestnuts were eaten and the shells were burning away on the fire, the children went to brush their teeth, and get ready for prayers and bed.

* * *

The next morning when the children went out to attend to their morning chores, they were surprised to find a visitor waiting outside the front gate of the farmhouse. Leezah was carrying the pig scrap bucket and Olingah was carrying the container for the eggs, as they came around the corner of the house.

"Joey!" exclaimed Olingah. "What are you doing here?"

When Skye opened the gate, the joey hopped through and immediately began to snuffle at Olingah.

"Hullo Joey," Olingah's voice was full of delight. "Did you miss us too?" He gave the wallaby a rub between the ears.

"Come on Olly," called Leezah, "It's chore time. We can talk with Mummy and Daddy about Joey later."

"Bye Joey," said Olingah reluctantly.

As Olingah followed his sisters across the field to the pig pen, Joey followed. When Olingah turned and saw the wallaby following behind them, he started to laugh. After the children left the pig pen and walked up the hill to the shed to feed the farm dogs, Joey hopped after them. And sure enough, as they headed down the hill to the hen house, to let the hens out and collect the eggs, Joey came along behind. Olingah was thrilled.

When they arrived back at the farmhouse, Flea Flex and Fizz were at the front gate. Now that the joey was no longer kept in the front garden, the puppies were free to roam all over the front and back garden. But the wallaby was not at all afraid of them. When the gate was opened he happily hopped through, back to his old home. Though the puppies were running around and occasionally came up and sniffed him, he seemed to be perfectly at ease. He followed the children and the puppies up the side of the house and came into the back yard.

Flip and Rommy were hanging some washing as the children, puppies and wallaby came in to the back yard. "Look Mummy! Joey wants to live with us!" said Olly. Rommy and Flip looked over at the wallaby. Rommy looked at Flip. Flip shrugged his shoulders. "You da boss," he said with a grin. Rommy went back to hanging washing. Olly hoped if no one talked about it, the joey would stay, so he didn't say anything more. The children got ready to go to school and went to wait for the bus.

When Wayne got on the bus, the first thing he asked Leezah was, "Do you have the

PowerPoint presentation?" Leezah grinned and nodded.

"Do you have the container with dirt and gems?" she asked him back. He also nodded.

At school they went straight to the classroom. Some other students were there huddled around the heater at the back of the room. Their teacher was at her desk marking some homework.

"Good morning Wayne and Leezah," she said as the students approached her desk. "Are you ready for your presentation this morning?"

"Yes, we are," said Leezah. "Here's the memory stick with the presentation." The teacher took the memory stick and plugged it in to her computer. There were no problems with the pictures or the sound.

"Great, when the bell goes, you can start," the teacher said.

Leezah and Wayne waited for the rest of the group to arrive. They gathered in a corner of the classroom and chattered about the presentation. Everyone was feeling nervous. Leezah was repeating a prayer to herself.

When the bell rang, the other students took their seats at their desks. The junior youth group stood at the front of the classroom, ready to start. Just before they started, Ms Vermeer arrived.

"I'd like to see it too, if that's okay," she said, and walked to the back of the classroom. The junior youth suddenly felt twice as nervous!

Wayne started the presentation by asking the class what they could see in the bowl. Then he passed the bowl around so the students could dig in the soil. Straight away the attention of all the students was fully focused on the presentation. Each junior youth gave their part of the presentation. Sometimes they forgot what they were going to say. But the other members of the group came to their rescue.

At the end, the class clapped loudly. Leezah handed out the registration forms and invited anyone who wanted to join a junior youth group to fill out the form. All of Wayne's friends and most of the rest of the class took a registration form. Leezah felt like the junior youth group had been hit by the gales of confirmation.

BOOK FOURTEEN

FLYING FITZGERALDS

In the fourteenth book of the Fellowship Farm series Olingah has a close encounter with a million maggots. Leezah receives an exciting letter but struggles to be generous in prosperity. As a result of the letter, the family has opportunity to go on a journey. The journey takes them to a place of unlimited sweets, where Olingah and Skye-Maree learn some important truths from the strawberries dipped in chocolate, pavlova, cake, ice-cream, and doughnuts.

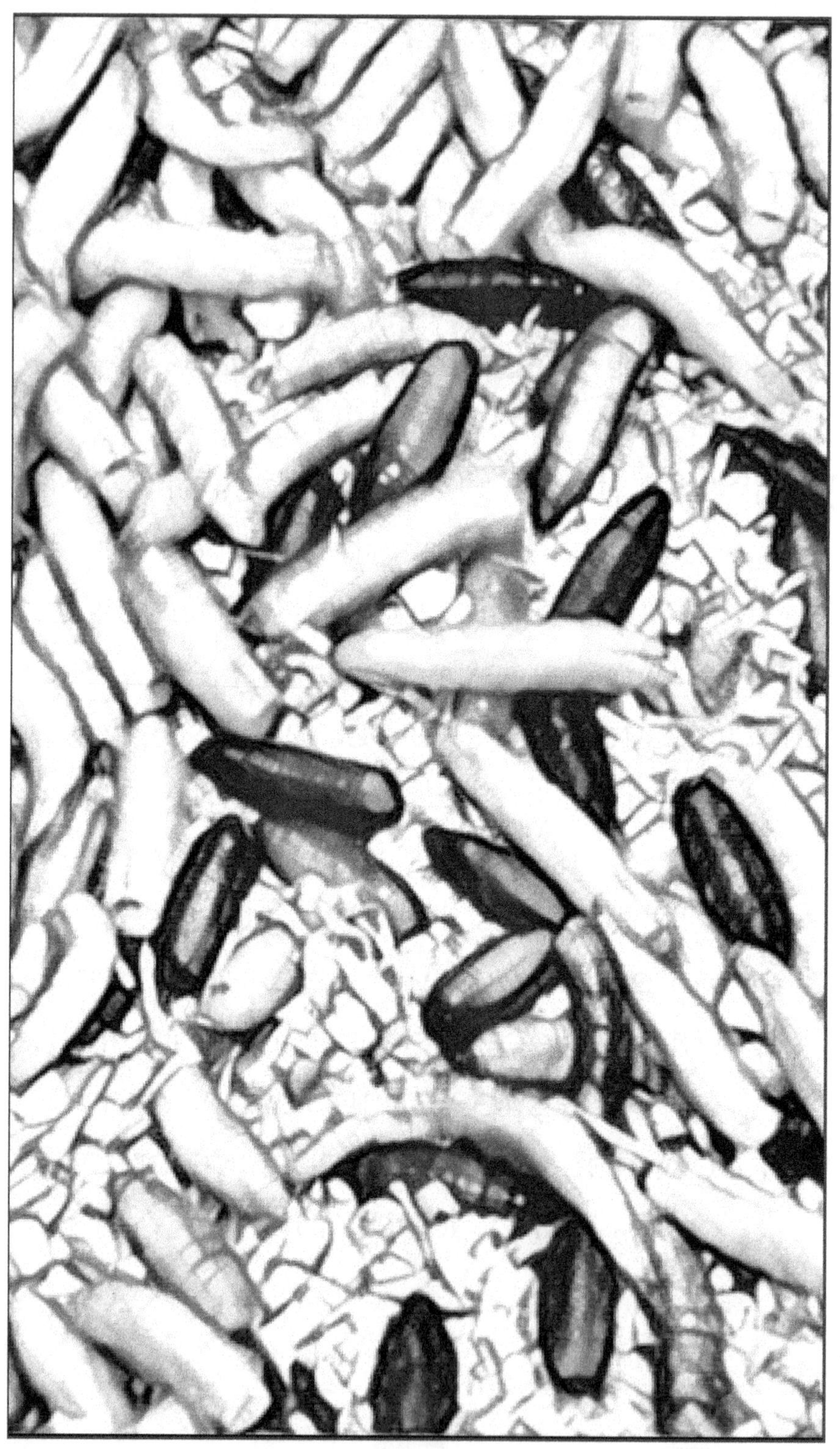

Munching maggots

The winter rain fell from the night sky on the farmhouse as the Fitzgeralds of Fellowship Farm prepared for the first day of term three. Leezah was eleven and was in year six. Her nine-year-old sister Skye-Maree was in year four. Their seven-year-old brother, Olingah, was in year two. They all went to Kellyton primary school. It had been a very cold and wet July holidays, and the children were looking forward to returning to school.

They spent the evening making sure their uniforms, books, and bags were ready for school. Rommy was making sandwiches for their lunches when she noticed that Olingah's lunch box was missing.

"Where is it Olly?"

"I don't know Mummy."

"Check your bag in the boot room," suggested Rommy.

Olingah went out onto the veranda and into the boot room. He turned on the light. Leezah's bag and Skye's bag were hanging on the bag hooks by the door. Olingah's bag was in the back corner of the boot room where he had thrown it in his excitement about holidays, at the end of the last day of term two.

He went over to it and picked it up. He noticed a lot of movement when he picked up the bag. Suddenly he realised the movement came from thousands of ants and hundreds of maggots. They were crawling and wriggling in his bag, on his bag, and on the floor around his bag. There was a very strong bad smell.

"YUCK!" Olingah shouted and dropped his bag.

He hurried back to the kitchen.

"Mum, I found my lunchbox."

"Well done. May I please have it?"

"Um. Nope. It's full of ants and maggots and it stinks."

Rommy handed Olinga a scrubbing cloth and the bottle of washing up liquid.

"Here you are my love. Go and clean your box, your bag, and the floor of the boot room please."

"Oh no Mum! It stinks! I can't touch it Mum!" cried Olingah.

"Who is going to clean it then Olly?" Rommy asked, smiling lovingly at him.

"Oh Mum! Can't you? Please Mum!"

Rommy handed Olingah some rubber gloves. "You can wear these if you like."

Olingah took the gloves, cloth and detergent. He went back to the boot room and put on his boots. He felt sick at the smell and sight of all the maggots.

"This is DIS.GUS.TING!" he said aloud to himself.

He slipped on the rubber gloves. They were way too big for his little hands but it was better than touching maggots.

Olingah lifted the bag, with ants and maggots dropping off it along the floor. He carried it along the veranda to the outside sink. He dropped it in the sink. Scores of little white wrigglers fell off the bag and into the sink. They immediately started to wriggle their way to the edges of the sink. "This is DIS.GUS.TING!" Olingah said again as the smell of rotting food and maggots wafted up his nostrils. A few tears sprung from his eyes.

He turned on the tap and the water started to wash the creepy crawlies down the sink. Olingah turned his bag slowly round and round, letting the water run down the sides. Then he opened the zipper as much as he could. He pulled the sides of the bag down.

Inside the bag was the lunchbox. Inside the half-open lunch box was the last of a rotten apple core and left over cheese sandwich, barely recognisable through the wriggling, crawling cover of black and white. Olingah tried not to breathe in, as he pulled the box out of the bag, and emptied the contents onto the lawn. He then dropped the box under the tap. It took a long time to rinse the bag and box completely clean.

Olingah dumped the wet bag on the veranda, hoping it would dry somehow. He then used the scrubber and the detergent to thoroughly clean his lunchbox. When he had washed and rinsed his lunchbox, he dropped his boots to the bootroom and went back into the kitchen.

Rommy had his lunch on the table ready to put in the box. She smiled as he came in.

"How is it?" she asked.

"DIS.GUS.TING!" frowned Olingah. "I feel sick in my stomach."

"Well done for cleaning your lunch box and bag Olly."

"It doesn't feel well done," said Olingah crossly, "It feels disgusting."

Rommy continued to smile at Olingah as she dried the box with a tea towel. "It sounds like you didn't enjoy cleaning maggots out of your bag and lunch box Olly?"

Olingah looked at Rommy with a frown, but he didn't have anything more to say.

"Please go and get ready for bed now," Rommy said, "We will have evening prayers in ten minutes."

After prayers, Flip took himself off to bed. Leezah and Skye-Maree read by the fire, and Rommy settled Olingah in bed. As he burrowed under his doona like a little wombat, he said to his mother: "Don't you love me as much as you did when I was six?"

Rommy was surprised by the question.

"Of course I love you just as much as when you were six my darling," she replied. "And I will love you when you are eight, nine, ten, twenty, thirty-five, sixty-one, a hundred and eleven!"

"Mummy even I won't be alive when I'm a hundred and eleven and neither will you!"

"I will always love you Olly, just the same as I have always loved you! Why do you ask?"

"Because when I was six and I left my lunchbox in my bag over the holidays, and the cockroaches got into it, you cleaned it for me. But now I'm seven, you made me do it. And it was revolting. So if you loved me the same as before you would have cleaned my lunch box for me. But you didn't."

Rommy gave Olingah a big kiss and a hug. Then she answered him.

"`Abdul'-Bahá says that mummies and daddies should 'accustom [their children] to hardship'. If we make everything easy for you, you don't learn responsibility. It feels easier to have someone clean your smelly bag, but if we keep doing that, you don't learn anything. Do you think you will ever leave your lunch box in your bag again Olly?"

"NO WAY!" said Olingah.

"So, you have grown my love. You have learned to be more responsible. Tomorrow you can put three stickers on the virtues chart next to 'responsibility', to celebrate that growth."

Olingah closed his eyes and curled up in a ball. He didn't like being accustomed to hardship, at all. Rommy kissed him good night.

Fighting, fairness and forgiveness

When the children got off the school bus after their first day of term three, the winter rain was pouring, but Leezah stopped to open the flap on the green mailbox out the front of Fellowship Farm. Leezah had been checking the post every Monday since she sent off the labels from two pineapple tins, with the hope of winning a family cruise. The postbox was empty. The children waded from the gate to the house and went inside to have their afternoon snacks before going out on the farm to do chores with their dad.

While they ate at the small table in the kitchen, the children heard the sound they had been waiting for. It was the sound of a motorbike engine. It came up the road and stopped outside the farm for a moment. A few seconds later the children heard the beep beep of the motorbike horn. The motorbike then turned around and headed back down the wet and potholed road.

"The postman has come!" cried Leezah, dropping her unfinished sandwich on her plate. She jumped up, and rushed through the kitchen door and out to the back veranda. At the other end of the small kitchen table, Olingah struggled to stand. He urgently wanted to go and check the mail too. "Wait! Wait for me!" Olingah wailed. But Leezah was already in the boot room, pulling on her raincoat, rain hat and boots. Olingah dropped his sandwich and ran after his sister.

The puppies were thrilled to see Leezah and came splashing across the flooded back lawn and up the steps on to the back veranda. When they arrived under the shelter they shook their wet bodies vigorously, sending a spray of wet-dog-smelling water all over Leezah. "Ugh, you gooses!" she laughed, and stomped down the path, which was now more like a shallow stream.

The land between the front gate of the farm house and the front gate of the farm was covered in water. Leezah and the puppies splashed their way through to get to the mailbox. The mail was in a large plastic bag, inside the mailbox. Leezah grabbed it and turned to go back to the farm house. Olingah was just coming down the path by the side of the house. "Come on Olly. Let's go!" Leezah shouted over the noise of the rain and the wind as she gently pushed him back the way he had come.

The children hung their wet coats, hats, and boots to dry in the boot room. The puppies tumbled around on the veranda, while Leezah and Olingah hurried back into the warm house.

Leezah took the dripping plastic bag to the dining table in the living room. She dried it down with a tea towel before opening it up and tipping all the mail onto the table. There were bills and other official looking letters, all addressed to Flip or Rommy. There was a letter from Kellyton Primary School, and a postcard for Rommy. But there didn't seem to be anything from the Sunshine Australia Fruit Company. There was nothing addressed to Leezah. Leezah and Olingah were disappointed. They stacked the other mail neatly at the end of the table, and hung the plastic bag to dry above the kitchen sink.

As they stacked the mail, Leezah noticed an official-looking envelope addressed to Ms E.

Fitzgerald. "Wait!" cried Leezah. "That's me! E. Fitzgerald. Ms Elizabeth Fitzgerald". Leezah tore open the envelope while her siblings watched with bated breath. There was a piece of paper inside. At the top of the page there was a golden pineapple and the words Sunshine Australia Fruit Company Pty Ltd.. Leezah started to read the letter, then suddenly yelled "Yipeee!" Skye-Maree and Olingah started bouncing on the spot.

"What?!" they asked, "What does it say?"

Leezah started to dance. "We. Are. Going. On. A." Leezah stopped dancing, and grinned.

"A what Leezah a what??" cried Olingah.

"A croooooooooooooooooz!!" Leezah finished. She passed the letter to her siblings.

It was way too difficult for Olingah, and Skye also struggled to understand the official text of the letter but they could see the big gold letters saying 'Congratulations!' Just then there was a honk out the front of the farm house. Flip had come to get the children for their afternoon chores.

"Oh no! We haven't even changed yet!"

The children spoke to Flip on the radio to let him know they would be out in two minutes. Then they rushed off to their bedroom to change into their farm clothes. Everyone was racing to put their clothes on, partly because they didn't want to keep Flip waiting, and partly because each one wanted to be the one who told Flip the news about the cruise.

"I want to tell Daddy," said Olingah, pulling on his pants so quickly that he didn't notice at first that they were back to front.

"No, I want to," said Leezah, rushing to turn the sleeves of her jumper in the right way so she could pull it on.

"NO!" said Olingah. "LET ME!"

"But I was the one who entered the competition Olly. That's not fair."

Olingah pulled his socks on and ran through the bedroom door.

"Don't you dare!" Leezah yelled after him. She chased him and grabbed his arm, yanking it back so that Olingah couldn't run off to put his boots on. Olingah cried out in pain and fell onto the floor. Leezah rushed past him, through the kitchen and out to the boot room. She pulled on her boots and hat, and ran down the side of the farmhouse to the white Ute. She pulled open the door of the Ute and said, "GUESS WHAT DADDY?"

Before Flip even had a chance to guess, Leezah continued, "We won the cruise!" Flip raised his eyebrows and wiggled his ears. He raised his hand to high-five his daughter. Leezah climbed into the Ute. Just as she shut the door, she saw Olingah coming slowly down the path in the rain with Skye's arm around his shoulder. It was clear from the look on his face that he was crying, though the tears streaming down his face mingled with the rain. He was clutching the arm that Leezah had yanked.

Skye-Maree opened the back door of the Ute and helped her brother in. His shoulder was very sore so Skye helped him with his seat belt. Leezah sat very still and quiet on the front seat, looking straight ahead.

"What happened to my boy?" asked Flip unclipping his seat belt and turning to face the back seat.

"Leezah broke my arm," sniffed Olingah.

Flip looked at Leezah. His eyebrows were raised again, but this time his ears were not wiggling. Leezah ignored his stare and looked straight out the front window, which was starting to fog up from their breath. Flip turned his attention back to his son.

"Where is it broken sonshine?" he asked.

"In my shoulder," sniffed Olingah as the tears dried up.

"Do you think you should give the chores a miss today Olly?" asked Flip. Olingah nodded. "And perhaps you had better stay and take care of him Skye-Maree," Flip continued. "Perhaps Leezah can work alone today."

Leezah continued to look straight ahead in silence as Skye-Maree and Olingah climbed back out of the car and walked slowly back to the farmhouse. Flip started the engine and drove up toward the hay barn.

As they drove along, Flip was also silent. The only sound was the wind screen wipers swishing back and forth. There was a big hole which was usually filled with Flip's questions about the day at school, and with funny jokes. As they drove in silence, and pushed the hay onto the Ute in silence, and attended to all the chores in silence, Leezah thought.

She thought about winning the cruise. She thought about scrambling into her clothes so she could be the first one to tell Flip. She thought about Olingah yelling that he wanted to be the one to tell Flip. She thought again that it was only fair that she should tell her dad, as she was the one who entered the competition. She thought Olingah was very very annoying. She thought he wasn't fair. She thought he always wants his own way. These thoughts went around and around in Leezah's head.

But as time passed and the chores continued in silence, Leezah could not help thinking about what she had done to her brother. She remembered how she had grabbed his little arm in her strong hand. She remembered how she had pulled it hard and yanked him to the ground. She thought about how she had left her brother on the floor and run off. She thought about the pain he was in, and the tears streaming down his face. She thought about how she had not said sorry when he got in the car.

Tears started to roll down her face. Leezah started to wonder if being the one to tell Flip about the cruise was worth the suffering she had caused her brother. She started to wonder what she could have done differently.

When the chores were almost finished, Flip parked the Ute and they walked in silence past the hen house, collected the eggs, and continued home. The rain was easing and the tears had dried on Leezah's cheeks.

She had an idea of what she could have done. She thought it was fair that she wanted to be the one to tell Flip about the cruise. But if Olingah didn't respect that, she should not have grabbed his arm. She thought it would have been better to let him get to Flip first, and then they could have discussed it as a family later. Maybe through consultation Olingah would have seen that what he had done wasn't fair, and he would have made a different choice next time.

Just as they went through the gate, Flip put his arm around Leezah and gave her a big hug. He kissed the top of her head, and then they went inside.

Rudey nudey risk

When Flip and Leezah entered the kitchen, they noticed that the faces of Rommy, Skye-Maree, and Olingah were rather glum. The letter from the fruit company was open on the kitchen table. Leezah felt ashamed. She walked over to her brother and wrapped him in her arms, taking care not to press his right shoulder. "I'm very sorry Olly. I shouldn't have hurt you. It was unkind of me."

"That's okay Leezah," said Olingah.

"Thank you for your humility Leezah, and your forgiveness Olly. You may both put stickers on the virtues chart. But I'm afraid we have some disappointing news Leezah."

Leezah turned to look at her mother.

"The letter doesn't say we won a cruise darling."

Leezah's face fell. "Oh. What does it say?"

"It says that in the competition for the cruise, we won a secondary prize."

"What's a secondary prize? What did we win?" asked Leezah.

"We won a year's supply of tinned pineapple."

"Oh no," moaned Flip. "I think I've just gone right off pineapple."

Rommy picked up the letter and glanced at it again.

"However, apart from all that pineapple, there is something that you will be happy about. The prizes are presented in Sydney, and the company will fly our family to Sydney for the award ceremony."

"So we get to go to Sydney?" grinned Leezah.

"Yes, so long as we agree to have our photo in the paper holding the certificate from the fruit company!"

"I agree!" said Leezah.

"I agree!" said Skye-Maree.

"I agree!" said Olingah.

"Well, in two weeks' time we will go to Sydney. We had better check that you three have some respectable clothes to wear. It will be warmer up there than in Kellyton."

* * * * *

Two weeks later on Friday, Flip picked the children up from school at lunchtime. He parked the car across the road from the school. Together they walked across the road and down the street toward the op-shop. As usual, Sue was inside. Whenever she wasn't busy hanging new donations, she worked on her quilts, which she made by hand. Her mouth was full of pins when the family came in. She waved hullo and took the pins from her mouth, sticking them carefully into her echidna-shaped pin cushion. "Hullo Fitzgerald four," she smiled, "What can I do for you today?"

"We are going to Sydney!" said Olingah jumping on the spot. "We need to get some reespeckable clothes because its warmer in Sydney and we've grown!" he explained.

Sue's face folded into wrinkles of concern. "Ooooh," she said, "I haven't got much spring stock. It's been so cold. People are still buying winter gear."

It was true. The children looked around the shop. There were only a few pairs of shorts – which looked like they were for very large ladies.

"Sorry," Sue apologised.

"That's okay Sue," said Flip with a serious face, "the children can just run around Sydney rudey nudey."

Sue looked shocked, and Leezah started to giggle.

After the family left the shop, they drove back to the farm. They radioed Rommy to let her know they had not found anything at the op-shop and were on their way home. When they got home, Rommy was serving bowls of pasta with pesto and cheese on top. They would be travelling that evening, so Rommy wanted to make sure they had a good hot meal for lunch.

After lunch Rommy and Flip asked the children to rummage through the plastic boxes at the bottom of their wardrobe. The boxes held their cooler clothes. They had not worn them for months. They pulled out their lighter pants and shirts. But the children had been busy growing over the past six months and nearly everything was too small. Skye-Maree tried on a shirt that had been her favourite last spring. It was so small that she got stuck in it. Leezah and Olingah had to yank it over her head to get it off. "I guess that t-shirt is now yours Olly!" she said, passing it to him.

The children took their toothbrushes and hairbrushes from the bathroom, a couple of books each, a prayer book, pyjamas and some underwear. They dropped them into the empty suitcase that Rommy and Flip had laid out in the living room.

"Is that all?" asked Rommy.

"Yep," said Leezah, as Olingah dropped some of the shirts his sister had handed down to him, into the case. "Nothing fits us anymore!"

"There's a problem here," said Flip.

"Yes!" agreed Rommy.

"And I have the solution," continued Flip.

"Great!" exclaimed Rommy looking hopeful.

"The problem is our children keep growing. The solution is we have to stop feeding them."

Rommy stopped looking hopeful. Flip continued: "If we reduce their rations to one meal per week, we will not have to buy clothes every year."

"True story Sherlock," said Rommy, "but let's explore other options first."

Rommy went into the kitchen, picked up the phone and pressed the buttons. After a short pause the children heard her say: "Hi Annissa, it's Aunty Rommy here. Yes! We will see you tonight. Yes! We are very excited about it too. Thank you darling. Yes. Lovely. Yes, could I please talk with Mummy or Daddy? Thank you."

There was a brief pause, then: "Jen! Hi! Yes, we're just packing now. I know. We left it to the last minute. We thought it would be quick and easy. But we have just realised that the children have literally no suitable clothes! Nothing fits! And the op-shop is still selling heavy winter clothes as it's still freezing down here." There was a pause, then, "Bless you Jen. Thank you! See you tonight! Bye!"

Rommy looked relieved. "Ok. Problem solved. Children can keep eating," she said, glancing at Flip.

"Phew," said Flip.

"Jen is going to take us to the shopping centre in Chatswood tomorrow before we go to the award ceremony. We will pick up some presentable clothes." The children looked at each other with big grins. They couldn't remember ever going to a shopping centre before, and they very rarely bought new clothes. Tomorrow sounded like a fun adventure.

Rommy and Flip packed their own clothes. Flip and the children made some sandwiches, a thermos of hot chocolate, and packed some fruit and muesli bars. Just as they finished, the children heard a sound that filled their hearts with joy. It was the sound of Ruha's van pulling in to the farm. The children rushed outside and yanked on their gumboots. They ran down the side of the house to where Ruha was just pulling a zip-up bag of belongings from the back seat. She was nearly knocked off her feet with the loving hugs of Olingah, Skye and Leezah.

Ruha was going to stay at Fellowship Farm for the weekend. She would earn some pocket money taking care of the domestic animals and keeping an eye on the farm. "Hullo my gorjusses," she cried, her brown eyes sparkling with love.

As if in the embrace of an octopus, Ruha walked slowly up the side of the house. She had already had a tour of the farm and practiced feeding all the animals. The children showed her to the spare room where Ruha would sleep. Rommy gave her the key to the white Ute, and the house.

When Ruha was settled, the family took their almost empty case to the orange Ute. The children gave the puppies one last good bye cuddle. Then it was Ruha's turn. After squeezing Ruha like a toothpaste tube, it was time to pile into the Ute. Ruha waved the family good bye, grinning from ear to ear. She shut the farm gate behind them and the Fitzgerald family headed down the dirt road to Kellyton.

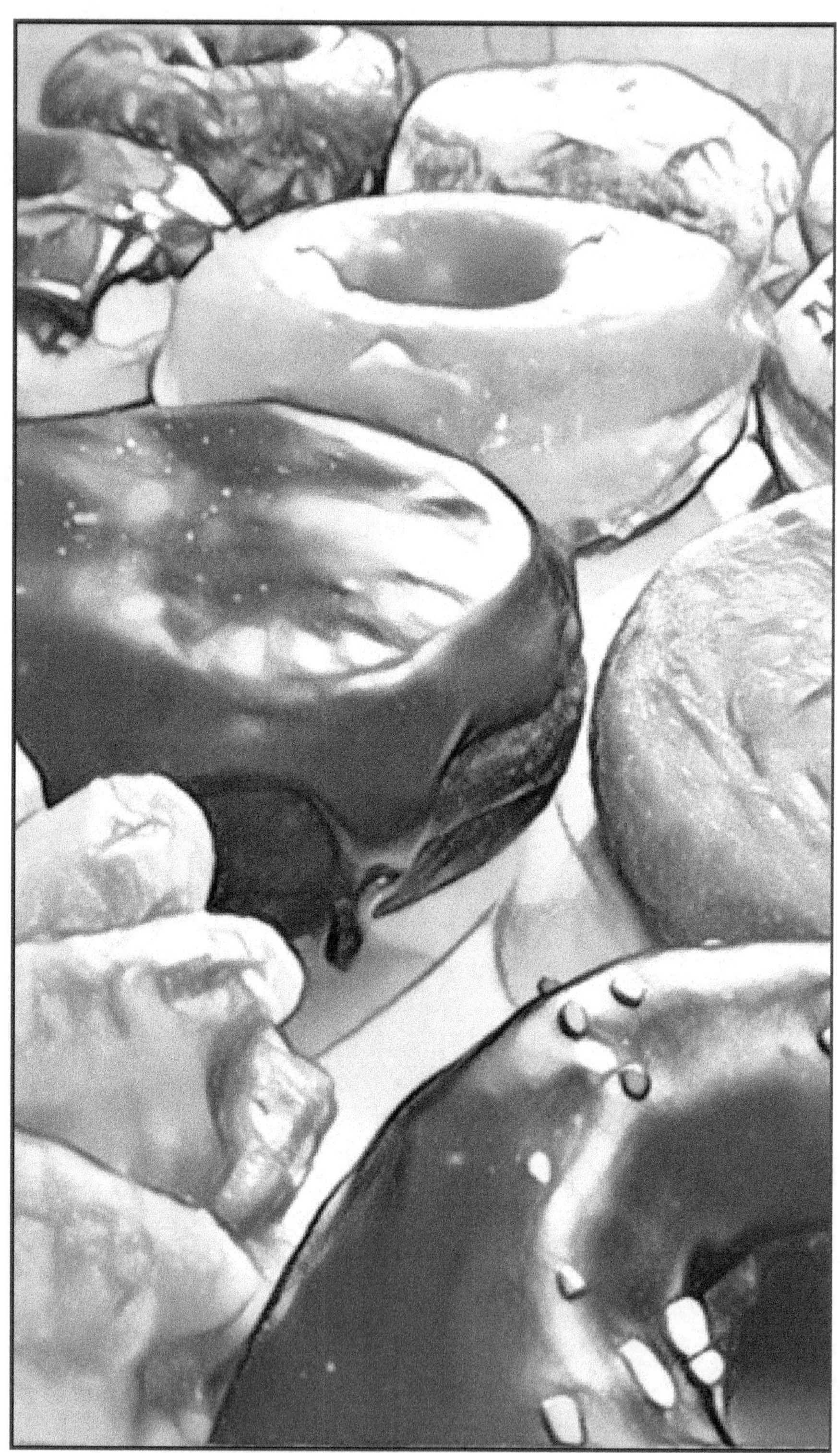

Fear, faith, and flashy frosting

As they drove the two hours to Launceston, Skye focused on the clouds far off in the sky so as to avoid car sickness. Leezah read a book. Olingah, seated in the middle of the back seat, was focused on the road and the dashboard. He would note the speed limit signs and then check what speed the Ute was travelling. He kept checking the fuel gauge to see if petrol was low. He squeezed his eyes shut when a car passed them on either side of the road.

Glancing at him in the rear view mirror, Flip noticed that Olingah seemed anxious. "How are you feeling son?" asked Flip.

"Fine," said Olingah. Just then a car passed them on the opposite side of the road. Olingah closed his eyes tightly.

"Why are you closing your eyes Olly?" Flip asked.

Olingah was quiet for a minute. He was thinking about the question. At first he wasn't really sure why he was closing his eyes.

"I don't want anything bad to happen," he said eventually.

"Why do you think something 'bad' might happen?" asked Rommy.

"Well, when we went to Launceston to pick up Annissa and Nick we got a smashed window and a flat tyre. Then when we went skiing, we saw a wallaby get hit by a car. I'm just worried something bad will happen this time too."

"Nothing bad will happen Olly," said Leezah.

"Well, we don't know what might happen," replied Rommy, thoughtfully. "Lots of things could happen. And something could happen that is very challenging or scary. But we don't need to worry about them because we have faith."

"Faith that Bahá'u'lláh won't let bad things happen?" asked Olingah.

"No, faith that Bahá'u'lláh will always give us the strength to deal with anything that comes along," Rommy clarified.

"We need to make good choices Olly," said Flip. "So we make sure the car's engine is taken care of. We fill it with petrol. We put good tyres on the car. We obey the speed zones. We concentrate when we drive. We don't drive when we are tired or sick. But then we can relax. We can trust that whatever comes our way, God will give us the strength to manage it."

"Ok," said Olingah.

"And if we lose confidence sometimes, it's a good time to pray," added Rommy.

"Ok," said Olingah again. He wasn't sure he felt confident that he could manage if something 'bad' happened. He decided to say some prayers quietly to himself. He sat back against the seat and closed his eyes. Inside his head, Olingah sang "O God! Refresh and gladden my spirit, purify my heart, illumine my powers..." As he sang the prayer over and over in his head, he started to feel relaxed. Eventually, Olingah became so relaxed that he fell fast asleep.

The sun was setting when the Fitzgerald family pulled up at the long term car park of the Launceston airport. Leezah woke Olingah, and everyone climbed out of the Ute. Skye pulled the suitcase. Flip carried the carry bag with the food and thermos.

They followed the path from the car park to the terminal. Big colourful feet were painted all along the path between the car park and the terminal. Olingah jumped from painted foot to painted foot, all the way along. As they arrived at the terminal, the glass doors slid open. The family stepped gratefully out of the cold wintry air into the warmth of the heated building.

They joined the line of travellers at the Greenways Air counter. The children watched as each customer put their case on the conveyor belt for weighing. The suitcase was then trundled away on the conveyor belt, and went through a curtained hole. Olingah wondered where the bags went. When it was their turn, they put the case on the scale next to the counter.

"Goodness! You travel lightly!" smiled the air hostess. Her hair was pulled back tightly from her face into a neat bun, and she had very red lips. "This suitcase only weighs 4kg!"

"We wanted to leave plenty of space in case we need to pack one of the children away," said Flip with a serious face.

"I see," said the hostess, continuing to smile with her very red lips.

She passed five pieces of cardboard to Rommy. "These are your boarding passes Dr Fitzgerald. You will be boarding through Gate 2 at 7pm."

Rommy took the boarding passes and smiled thank you.

The children were yearning to go and explore the little airport. They had been there many times before to welcome or farewell friends and relatives. It was really just one very large room. There were no escalators or hallways to explore and not many shops. But it was always fun to see the displays of the old planes, wander around the book and gift shop, look at the pastries and sandwiches for sale in the café, and run up and down the tiled floor of the terminal building.

"Can we explore?" asked Skye-Maree.

Flip nodded. "You may. We'll be in the gate lounge. Come and join us when you're hungry. And remember we will be boarding in an hour, so don't get lost or we'll have to leave without you."

The children ran off.

There were all the usual things to see in the airport but there was also something new. Next to the café was a glass display case full of doughnuts. The children counted them all. There were 66 different types! They read the name labels and had a long discussion about which one they would eat if they could have one each.

There were chocolate, strawberry, lemon flavoured doughnuts; doughnuts with cream, custard, icing sugar; mini doughnuts and mega doughnuts; doughnuts with coloured sprinkles and doughnuts with blueberries; doughnuts of every colour and flavour! After looking at them and talking about them for a long time, the children realised they were hungry.

Through the glass wall they could see Rommy and Flip in the gate lounge. They were sitting near the front window, eating sandwiches and drinking hot chocolate. The whole front wall of the terminal was one big window. During the day, people waiting for planes could see the tarmac and watch the planes landing and taking off. The children went through the security arch and joined their parents in the gate lounge.

"I'm starving!" announced Skye-Maree.

"You've come to the right place then," said Rommy, and offered each of them a sandwich.

The children each ate two sandwiches, a pear, a muesli bar and a cup of hot chocolate. While they ate, they described the doughnuts they had seen.

"Can we please buy one?" asked Olingah. "They are only $4 each."

"But why would we pay someone $4 to poison you, when we can poison you ourselves for free?" asked Flip.

"Daaaad!" moaned Olingah. "It's not poison, it's food. Yummy food!"

"You know what?" said Rommy, "I have a feeling there will be plenty of yummy poisonous food at the award ceremony, and you may be allowed to eat some of it. So let's go wash our hands and brush our teeth and get ready to board the airplane!"

Just then, they heard an announcement: "Good evening ladies and gentlemen. This is the boarding call for passengers carrying valid boarding passes for Greenways Air flight GA 959 to Sydney. This flight will be boarding through Gate Two. We will be boarding the aircraft through the front and rear stairs this evening. Please ensure your mobile phones are switched to airplane mode before crossing the tarmac. Thank you."

"That's our flight! That's our flight!" said Leezah excitedly. Rommy nodded and gave each of the children a boarding pass. Flip packed the empty lunchboxes and thermos into the carry bag. The Fitzgerald family lined up behind the other passengers. The air steward checked each boarding pass with a scanner, similar to the one the librarian used at Kellyton library. "Thank you Mr Fitzgerald," she said to Olingah as she scanned his pass. Olingah grinned. This was followed by, "Thank you Ms Fitzgerald. Thank you Ms Fitzgerald. Thank you Dr Fitzgerald. Thank you Mr

Fitzgerald," as each of them had their pass scanned.

They walked down the cement steps, where Olingah had torn his Feast clothes on a previous visit to the airport, and out through a door onto the tarmac. The tarmac was lit by powerful lights that made it as bright as day. There were people wearing bright orange vests, loading suitcases onto the plane, and driving around on buggies. When the children looked up at the window of the plane, they could see the pilots getting ready. Just as Leezah looked up at the pilots, one of them looked out and saw Leezah.

"Look," said Leezah, waving. "See the pilot in the cockpit? She's waving to us." They climbed the metal stairs and went inside the plane. Once again they showed their boarding passes to an air steward. Olingah was disappointed that the second air steward didn't call him Mr Fitzgerald.

The aisle between the rows of seats was narrow and there were lots of people standing in it. Some were putting their hand luggage in the overhead lockers. Some were trying to squeeze between the seat and another passenger to get to their own seat. Some were helping children settle. But eventually the aisle cleared and the family made their way to row nine. There were three seats on either side of the aisle. Olingah, Skye-Maree and Leezah sat on one side, while Rommy and Flip sat on the other side.

When everyone was seated, the air stewards demonstrated the safety features of the aircraft. Olingah paid very close attention. He hoped the plane wouldn't crash. At the same time, sliding down a big yellow slide from the emergency exit sounded quite fun. He liked the idea of having a life vest with a whistle and a light. And, just like the air steward told them to, he counted the number of rows between row eight and the nearest exit. The nearest exit was at row 13 – four rows away.

Soon the plane was ready for take-off. It rolled slowly forward and turned away from the terminal. Then it turned slowly left. Soon it was going as fast as a car, then faster than a car. It got faster and faster and faster. The children were pushed back against their seats. Then suddenly! The plane lifted off the ground. It quickly rose up into the sky. Outside the window, the children could see the lights along the side of the highway, and then the lights of Launceston. Everything was getting smaller and smaller as the plane flew higher and higher.

* * * * *

When the plane landed at Sydney airport, it was two hours past Olingah's bedtime. With the excitement of the journey he had stayed awake, but he was very tired. It was even past Leezah and Skye-Maree's usual bed time and they were also feeling weary. When the plane came to a complete stop, the children unbuckled their seatbelts. The passengers waited patiently by their seats and in the aisles until the air stewards unlocked the doors. Then the passengers started to file out. Instead of going down stairs onto the tarmac the children found themselves in a carpeted tunnel. As they came out of the tunnel and into the gate lounge they were attacked!

Shocks and temptations

Their cousins, Annissa and Nick, along with their Aunty Jen and Uncle Karim wrapped Leezah, Skye and Olingah in tight hugs and squeezes and covered them with kisses. Rommy and Flip were also squeezed and kissed. Tears flowed and the air was full of Alláh'u'Abhá! Welcome! How was your flight? Look how big you are? Are you exhausted? Let's get your baggage.

All tiredness was forgotten!

Nick was now 12 years old and Annissa was the same age as Olingah – seven. The children chattered and laughed as they walked and ran along the wide corridors of the huge airport. As it was getting late, the airport was not overly crowded. Leaving the adults to walk more slowly behind, the children ran ahead to play on the travelators. When no one else was using them, the children ran the wrong away, against the flow of the travelator, to see if they could run faster than it. They all could.

They walked down a long set of steps and through some special folding doors. Then they looked for the baggage carousel with GA 959 on the screen above it. Nick found it first and they went to wait right near the curtain where the bags came out. Olingah was very curious to know what was going on behind that curtain.

Soon the suitcases started coming out, and after a minute the children spotted the almost empty Fitzgerald suitcase. Rommy had tied bright red ribbons to the handle so it would be easy to distinguish from all the other dark blue suitcases. Nick grabbed the suitcase. He nearly fell over backwards because it was so light and he had been expecting it to be heavy.

The two families continued their animated conversations all the way to the cars. Aunty Jen and Uncle Karim had brought both their cars so that they could fit everyone in. Olingah, Annissa, Rommy, and Aunty Jen went in one car. Skye-Maree, Leezah, Nick, Flip and Uncle Karim went in the other car.

The roads were wide and busy, with many lanes of traffic. Olingah wondered how his aunt knew where to go. The city was lit up with millions of lights and even at such a late hour there were people and cars everywhere. Normally Jen and Karim travelled from the airport to their home by going through a big tunnel under the harbour. But for the sake of their special guests they went over the Sydney Harbour Bridge. The children looked out the window to see the Opera House all lit up. There were boats covered in lights on the harbour. It looked magical.

After about 40 minutes of driving, the Fitzgeralds arrived at the home of their cousins. The children piled out of the cars and rushed inside. The house was two storeys high. It had carpet and rugs everywhere! And lots of very beautiful furniture. But there was no time to admire that. Nick and Annissa led the way up the carpeted staircase, bounding up the steps. They took Leezah and Skye into Annissa's room which had two extra beds made up. Then they took Olingah to Nick's room. Nick's room had a double bed and a mattress made up on the floor. "You can sleep with me Olly if you want to, or you can sleep on the mattress on the floor." Olingah flopped onto the mattress on the floor.

As soon as Olingah lay down, he felt suddenly and completely exhausted. One minute later when Rommy came upstairs, he was fast asleep. Rommy pulled off his shoes and rolled him under the covers in his clothes. She kissed him good night. The other children also soon settled for bed. They brushed their teeth in a very large bathroom. The walls were covered with mirrors, and the carpeted floor and silver towel rails were heated!

Evening prayers were very brief, and as soon as they finished, four tired children closed their eyes and fell fast asleep.

* * * * *

When the children awoke, the sun was high in the sky and shining brightly. The girls crossed the hall and joined the boys in Nick's room. For Nick and Annissa, the morning air felt cold, and Annissa hurried to pull Nick's doonah over her legs. For the Tasmanian cousins the air felt like summer! Olly joined everyone on the double bed and Nick pulled out a bag full of UNO cards from a drawer near his bed. There were at least three packs of UNO cards combined into one and the pile was very high. Nick dealt everyone 15 cards which was almost too many for Annissa and Olingah to manage. Then a very intense game of UNO began.

The children were still playing UNO when Uncle Karim came into the room.

"Anyone hungry for some breakfast?"

"YES!" the children replied. Nick gathered up the cards and everyone hurried downstairs to the kitchen. The kitchen seemed almost as big as the Fitzgeralds' whole house! In the middle of the kitchen was a large wooden island with cupboards underneath and stools along one side of it. There were large windows in three walls as well as the roof, so it was full of sunlight. And everything was made of wood. There were pot plants in all the corners and everything looked new and very clean. There was already bacon, sausages, eggs, and tomato frying, as well as toast under the grill. Flip and Karim were chopping fruit from a large bowl on the island.

When everything was ready the family gathered around the island on the high stools. Aunty Jen handed out plates to everyone. The cooked food was served on large platters in the middle of the island. There were also boxes of cereals and various kinds of milk.

"Can I serve you some bacon?" Aunty Jen asked Leezah.

"No thank you Aunty Jen, I would like some eggs and toast please," Leezah replied.

Then Aunty Jen offered the same to Skye-Maree but received the same reply.

"Olingah, you love bacon and sausages!" she turned to her nephew. "How much would you like?" But she received the same reply.

"What's going on?" asked Aunty Jen, offering bacon, sausages and eggs to the rest of the family.

"We are vegetarian now Aunty Jen," explained Olingah. Aunty Jen's eyebrows shot up.

"Oh! Since when?" Aunty Jen was very surprised.

"Since we realised that eating meat means killing animals. It was a few weeks ago wasn't it Mummy?"

"Oh! Well, are you sure I can't tempt you?"

The aroma of the bacon was actually very difficult to resist. It smelt delicious! Olingah could imagine the salty taste of the bacon on his tongue. He remembered how much he loved chomping down on the crunchy crackling.

But Olingah shook his head. He ate lots of eggs, toast, fruit, and cereal instead.

After breakfast, the nine family members washed their hands and gathered in the sun room. It was another large room, full of couches, chairs and cushions. There was a table in the middle onto which Uncle Karim placed several prayer books. The Fitzgeralds wished they had their guitar. The family read and sang prayers a cappella for a while. Rommy sang a special teaching prayer for their journey. When they finished, Uncle Karim put the books away in a special cupboard.

The children scurried upstairs to get dressed, brush teeth, make beds.

Getting gorjuss

It was a short walk from Aunty Jen's house to the train station. At the station, the family walked down a long flight of stairs to the platform. Nick and Annissa showed Olly, Leezah and Skye where to wait. They were going toward the city so they had to wait on Platform Two. Along the platform were benches on which to sit, and big glass cases with rows of chocolate bars, chips, and drinks inside.

There were lots of people everywhere. Hanging down from the roof was a television screen. It said the next train would be there in one minute. Skye-Maree started to count. One Mississippi. Two Mississippi. Three Mississippi. Just as she got to 56 Mississippi she saw the train coming around the bend. There was a honk of a horn, a squeaking of brakes and a rush of air as the train passed the station and drew to a stop.

The sliding doors of the train opened. Aunty Jen led everyone inside. Olingah noticed that the gap between the train and the platform was the just the right size for him to fall down! He stepped carefully over it. Aunty Jen led them up a small flight of stairs to the second storey of the train.

On the second storey there were rows of blue seats all facing the same direction. Nick grabbed a handle on top of one of the seats and pushed it forward. Suddenly there were two long seats facing each other! The family settled in to their seats together. They could see the platform through the big window of the train. The sign said GORDON.

"Let's make as many words as we can from GORDON," suggested Skye.

"Good," said Nick straight away.

"Nod," said Rommy.

"Don."

"God."

"Door."

"Ron."

"Rood and nood," said Olingah, giggling.

"You don't spell it like that Olly," said Skye.

"Oh," said Olingah.

"Drongo!" said Flip.

Olingah looked shocked that Flip had called him a drongo and tears sprung to his eyes. Flip saw his look of surprise and explained, "We can make the word drongo out of GORDON, sonshine!"

"Go," said Uncle Karim. It was the last word made from GORDON before the train did go.

The train pulled out of the station and gathered speed. From the window the children could see roads and cars, houses, trees, and people, whizzing past. They wanted the train ride to continue and were disappointed when they found out they had to get off only a few minutes later. "You will have a longer ride on the train this afternoon, when we go to Darling Harbour," said Uncle Karim.

As the train slowed and stopped, the people on the train lined up by the sliding doors. As soon as the doors opened, the crowd of passengers flowed out onto the new platform. There were more passengers waiting to get in, as soon as they could. The first place Aunty

Jen took them was a flower shop near the train platform.

She squatted down so that she was close to the faces of her children, nieces, and nephew. "When we shop today we will need to stay together, so no-one gets lost. If anyone gets separated and you can't find the rest of us, you need to ask for directions to the train station. Then, at the train station come to this flower shop."

She gave each of them a piece of paper with a phone number on it. "You can also ask someone to call this number. It is for my mobile phone." The serious face of Aunty Jen and the plans she was making made Olingah feel worried. He hoped that no one would get lost. He hoped nothing 'bad' would happen. When each of them had put the number in their pocket, Aunty Jen stood up. Then she said, "Now let's go worship at the church of consumerism!"

The family headed down some wide cement steps and along a busy footpath. There were shops everywhere selling medicine, shoes, sushi, art supplies, nail painting, musical instruments, chocolate, more things than they could even have imagined! There were musicians on the footpath playing music, cars honking, children crying, and the constant gentle beeping sound of the pedestrian lights.

At the corner, the family crossed to the other side of the street and entered into a large building. Inside the building it seemed quieter and people moved more slowly. There were lots of shops, and there was music playing. The children could smell perfume, baking bread, coffee, pizza. They walked past a shop selling products made from sheep skin. Leezah ran her hand over a big soft rug that was on a table near the door. It felt a lot softer than the wool of the sheep on the neighbour's farm.

Aunty Jen led them to a large, brightly lit shop. For the Fitzgeralds, it seemed like the shop was the same size as the whole of Kellyton! As Jen led them to the clothes section, they passed rows and rows of toys, books, plates, cups, towels, pillows, gardening tools...Then they came to a large area with racks and racks of children's clothes. "Now!" said Aunty Jen with a big grin. "Rommy and Flip pipe down. This is my treat." She turned to the children. "I want each of you to choose two outfits each – shirts, trousers or skirts, jumpers, cardigans, shoes, underwear, socks and stockings – whatever you decide. Two full sets each. We will be sitting on the benches near the checkout ready to buy them. Just come to us there when you have made your choices. Nick and Annissa will show you where the dressing rooms are."

"Thank you Aunty Jen!" said all three. "Thank you Uncle Karim!" They gave their aunt and uncle big hugs. Then Nick and Annissa grabbed their hands, "Come on let's go," they said.

"Stay together!" said Rommy, as she was lead to the front of the shop by her sister.

The children had never seen such an assortment of clothes in all shapes, colors and sizes. Nick and Annissa helped them choose clothes that fit, and looked good.

Leezah chose one outfit all in red. Red woollen hat, red blouse, red jumper, red skirt, red stockings, red shoes and a red scarf. Olingah chose some yellow checkered pants, a red jumper and a yellow scarf. The outfit made him look just like Rupert Bear from the comic he liked to read. Skye-Maree chose a long green velvety dress with a purple cardigan and black shoes.

When they had finished choosing their clothes, Nick and Annissa led them to the front of the shop where the four parents were sitting, talking and, as always, laughing.

When Aunty Jen saw them, she leaped up. "Well done! Well done!" she said looking over their choices. She took them to the self-serve checkout. Aunty Jen waved each item in front of a small screen that beeped. When all the clothes were in the carry bags that Aunty Jen had brought, she stuck her debit card into the machine and pressed the buttons. Soon the machine spat out a long white piece of paper with numbers on it. Aunty Jen put the receipt into her handbag and passed the carry bags to Nick and Leezah. She dropped all the plastic coat hangers into a big yellow plastic box next to the checkout.

The children wrapped their arms around their aunty and showed their gratitude through a long tight squeeze. "You are most welcome my darlings," she grinned.

Travel by train

Shopping for clothes was fun, but for Leezah, Skye and Olingah, the train ride home was even better. On the way back to Aunty Jen's house Leezah led the way into the train and up the steps. She pushed the seat forward so that the family could all sit together.

"You're a train travelling professional now ,daughter!" said Flip with admiration as he settled on the seat.

"What words can we make from CHATSWOOD?" asked Skye-Maree, looking at the sign outside the window.

"Chat!"

"Wood!"

"Hat."

"What."

The train had pulled out of the station and the children had to remember the letters in their head.

"Cat."

"Swat."

"Shod," said Rommy.

"What does shod mean Aunty Rommy?" asked Annissa.

"It means to fit with a shoe. You could say a horse was shod if it had a shoe put on, for example."

"Do," said Olingah, wanting the game to continue.

"Dots," said Leezah.

"Hood."

"Stood."

The train ride home was over too quickly, and soon the family was lined up at the sliding doors, waiting to get off. The children leapt out of the train, and up the steps of the station. Nick and Annissa were confident of the way home and, after carefully crossing at the lights, the children ran ahead.

Rommy and Flip, Jen and Karim were deep in conversation when they turned into the garden and walked up the path to the front of the house. Suddenly, from behind the bushes on either side of the path, five monsters leaped out. They roared loudly. Uncle Karim screamed in genuine shock. After recovering from being startled, Flip roared back, running after the monsters as they fled squealing into the garden.

When the monsters had been dealt with, the family made and ate a quick lunch. Then it was time for showers and getting dressed up in the new Feast clothes. Even the simplest task, like having a shower and getting dressed, was fun at Aunty Jen's house.

The huge bathroom with the mirrors and heated carpeted floor also had a shower with two shower heads. So, all the girls had a shower together.

Attached to the wall were ceramic containers with fancy writing on them. One said Shampoo. Another said Conditioner. A third said Body Wash. The fourth said Foaming Face Cleanser. At the bottom of each container was a button. When the girls pressed the button, a little dollop of coloured liquid came out. Each liquid smelt like a different flower. By the time they had finished washing their faces, hair and bodies they smelt like a mixture of jasmine, rose, frangipani, and lavender.

While the boys had their showers, the girls dried off and dressed in their new clothes. Annissa had some Feast clothes too. When they were dressed they went into Aunty Jen and Uncle Karim's bedroom. Aunty Jen dried their hair with her hair dryer, making it warm, dry, soft and fluffy.

Just as she finished, the boys came into the bedroom, clean and dressed and smelling delicious. Aunty Jen dried their hair too, and soon everyone was looking very clean and very smart. Uncle Karim and Aunty Jen gave each child a dab of perfume, and then they were ready to go.

Just before they left the house for the train station, Uncle Karim set up a camera on the island in the kitchen. The family stood together, grinning from ear to ear and hugging each other while the camera went BEEP BEEP BEEP FLASH. When everyone had had a chance to look at the photo, the family headed out of the house and back to the train station.

This time the train journey took more than half an hour. The Fitzgerald children were thrilled. The very best part was when the train went over the Sydney Harbour Bridge. The water sparkled and the afternoon sun shone on the Opera House. There were yachts and ferries crossing the harbour.

"You know you can climb to the top of the bridge?" said Nick to his cousins who had their noses pressed against the window of the train.

"Really??" asked Skye, pulling her head back from the window and leaving a greasy mark. "That would be so much fun!"

"It is," said Nick, nodding. "My junior youth group climbed it this year," he added quietly.

"Really?" said Leezah. "My junior youth group just took care of smelly wet dog for a week," she added giggling.

"Serrr-vice. Service with a smile. Don't go being like a croc-o-dile." Nick was singing a song they all knew, and teasing his cousin for complaining about service. Leezah pretended to punch her cousin's arm.

Two stops later was Town Hall. It was a short walk from the station to Darling Harbour. There was a lot to see at Darling Harbour! No one wanted to hurry, but it was nearly time for the award ceremony to start. "You will have to come back one holidays and stay with us for a week," said Aunty Jen. The faces of the children lit up. Five heads nodded vigorously.

Aunty Jen led them to a fancy building with very high ceilings and glass walls - the Darling Harbour Art and Cultural Centre. At the front desk she explained what function they were looking for. The receptionist told them to take the escalators to the third floor and look for the Mish Elle Room. (The Mish Elle Room was named after the famous Australian pianist Mish and there was a photo of her at the entrance of the room.)

The Sunshine Australia Fruit Company had rented the room for the award ceremony. Inside the room were about ten large tables. Each one was covered in dark blue cloth and set for dinner. At each table there were ten very soft and comfortable chairs. Most of the tables were full. The family was greeted at the door and asked for a name. They were then shown to a table that had been reserved especially for them and had exactly nine seats around it. In front of the dining tables was a low stage. Along the wall were long tables covered in white table cloths and laden with food.

The family sat down and waited for the program to begin. They didn't have to wait long. But soon after the program started, the children hoped it would soon end. It was very boring.

There were speeches about the Sunshine Australia Fruit Company with lots of graphs and long words and numbers. Some television ads for the company were also shown. Finally, at the end, the family who won the cruise was called forward and issued with a certificate. They smiled a lot and had photos with the CEO of the company and were sent back to their seats. Then there was the awarding of the secondary prizes. The Fitzgerald family were called up to the stage and issued with their certificate promising them a year's supply of pineapple.

They also had photos, and then were sent back to their seats. But when the speeches were over and everyone had clapped and whistled, it was dinner time!

The children were very keen to get up from their seats and have a look at all the different types of food on the long tables. There were prawns and shell fish, curries and stews, many different coloured salads, rice, pasta, soups, crusty bread rolls, and much much more. But best of all was the dessert table. It was covered in cakes and pastries, ice-cream, pavlova, strawberries dipped in chocolate, and doughnuts just like the ones in the airport!

The children hurried back to their parents, who were still sitting at the table and had not yet gone to the buffet. "Mum!" cried Olingah. "WHAT are we allowed to eat?"

"Tonight you may all help yourself to whatever you like from the buffet. We strongly suggest you practice the virtues of moderation and self-discipline." The children could not believe their ears. The last words they heard were 'whatever you like from the buffet'. The words virtues, moderation, self-discipline floated on the air but didn't make it into the ears of the children.

Unfortunately.

Moderation goes missing

The first thing the children wanted to try was strawberries dipped in chocolate. Most of the other guests were helping themselves to dinner so there was no one at the dessert table. The children gathered around the table. They chose fat red juicy strawberries and dipped them, one by one, in a big heated dish of melted chocolate. The chocolate stuck to the strawberry making a smooth sweet creamy covering which then set. When each of them had a bowl full, they took their treats back to the table and sat up to eat them. The adults were at the buffet choosing some seafood and salads.

The children bit and licked the chocolate off the strawberries and then ate the strawberries. Olingah found that after the sweetness of the chocolate, the fruit didn't taste very sweet. After he had licked the chocolate off the strawberries and then licked the chocolate off his fingers, he left a few strawberries on his plate.

The next food to try was the doughnuts. There were rows and rows of them, just like behind the glass at the airport. They decided to choose two each. But Olingah couldn't decide between the doughnut with vanilla custard, the doughnut with caramel icing, and the doughnut covered in pink icing and hundreds and thousands. So he chose all three. They were delicious and very sweet. The children washed them down with some water.

Back at the dessert table Skye-Maree called everyone over to a soft-serve ice-cream dispenser. By pulling a handle, soft-serve ice-cream curved into their bowls. There were lots of containers nearby full of chocolate flakes, lolly pieces, and crushed nuts to sprinkle on top of the ice cream with little plastic spoons. Next to the ice-cream dispenser was another leaver that, when pulled, dispensed caramel or chocolate topping.

"Oh my goodness! Oh my goodness!" said Olingah jumping up and down as he watched his sisters and cousins dispensing the ice-cream and choosing their toppings. When it was his turn he wanted to try a bit of everything. Soon his bowl was nearly overflowing with chocolate ice-cream, strawberry ice-cream, vanilla ice-cream, ten different types of lollies and chocolates on top, and caramel sauce.

When the children took their sundaes up to the table, their parents were just finishing their main course. Rommy looked at her children's faces, covered in chocolate, and coloured icing, then she looked at the bowls full of ice-cream. She raised her eyebrows, turned to Uncle Karim, and continued her conversation.

Halfway through her bowl of ice-cream, Leezah realised she was completely full. She stopped eating. She could not eat one more spoonful of dessert. Everyone felt much the same, but Olingah and Skye could not bear to waste this very unusual opportunity. They kept eating their ice-cream until the spoon clinked on the bottom of the bowl.

When the ice-cream was eaten there was really no room for anything else in their tummies. "I just want to look," said Olingah. "Just to see what else there is."

"Me too," said Skye, holding her tummy with her hands.

The children all went back to the dessert table. They had not yet tried the custard tarts or pavlova or various types of cakes.

"Look Skye!" said Leezah, "It's Mississippi Mud Cake like Aunty Rae makes for the Nineteen Day Feast"

"Yum!" said Skye. "I just want a little bitty piece of it," she grinned, putting some of the rich chocolate cake on her plate.

"Oh! Look!" Olingah had spotted pink meringues shaped like pigs. He couldn't resist trying one. There was also cheese cake and caramel slice and fudge. Olingah couldn't resist trying just one each of those too.

Once again the children returned to the table. Nick, Annissa and Leezah drank some water while Skye-Maree and Olingah finished off their treats. Finally, even Olingah and Skye could not eat one more thing. Their faces and clothes were smeared with chocolate and coloured sugar. Leezah even had ice-cream on the end of one of her plaits.

The adults sipped some hot drinks while the children discussed how very full their tummies were. Soon after that, the guests started to leave. The Fitzgeralds and their cousins were feeling ready to leave as well.

The walk back to the train station seemed a lot longer than the walk from the train station. Skye and Olingah's tummies were so full it felt hard to breathe! By the time they got to the station it wasn't only that their skin felt stretched and their lungs felt cramped. Their tummies were starting to gurgle and grumble, squelch and slosh.

The cake and chocolate, doughnuts and ice-cream were starting to say that they didn't want to stay in these tummies much longer. By the time the train arrived at Gordon station, Olingah and Skye's brown complexions were looking very pale, even a shade of green. It was very difficult for them to walk along the platform and up the stairs.

Rommy and Flip helped them up and along the street to the house. When they arrived at Aunty Jen's house, she asked them to wait outside while she got some ice-cream containers. She was just in time.

Doughnuts, ice-cream, chocolate covered strawberries, Mississippi Mud Cake, and lollies came rushing out of Skye-Maree's mouth. A multi-coloured fountain of steaming half-digested food poured into the ice-cream container. Seeing Skye throw up was the last straw for Olingah, who was already feeling very unwell. A few seconds later he was kneeling on the cement path and spouting coloured soup into a second container. Flip and Rommy rubbed the backs of Skye and Olingah as tears rolled down the faces of the children. Each time they vomited it felt hard to breath.

Aunty Jen and Uncle Karim took the other children into the house. "Is anyone else feeling unwell?" she asked. The children shook their heads. Their tummies felt very full, but they didn't feel sick. "Good," said Aunty Jen with a smile. "Please go and get changed out of your Feast clothes. You could even put your pyjamas on." It was already dark and they were not planning to go out again.

When Olingah and Skye felt a little better, they came inside. They rinsed their mouths with water in the bathroom and brushed their teeth. Rommy and Flip helped them change out of their Feast clothes. As soon as they were in their pyjamas, they climbed into their beds. It was only seven o'clock. Aunty Jen put clean containers next to their beds in case they felt sick again.

Now that all the rubbish was out of their bodies, Olingah and Skye didn't feel like vomiting any more. They just felt very tired and their throats felt sore. Olingah curled up like a wombat, buried under the covers, and fell fast asleep. In the girls' room Skye-Maree tried to read one of her cousin's books before sleep, but after a few minutes, she was also fast asleep.

Rommy at risk?

Downstairs in the living room, Nick set up the Trivial Pursuit board. The family formed three teams: Rommy and Annissa; Nick and Aunty Jen; Leezah and Uncle Karim. Flip said he would be the referee in case things got heated and fights broke out.

"Dad, we don't need a referee in Trivial Pursuit," said Leezah. "How about you join our team?"

But Flip decided he would be the wild card. He would help all the teams answer the questions.

Nick rolled the dice and moved the green counter.

"It's a pity Olly and Skye miss out on our last night together," lamented Aunty Jen.

"Yes!" said Annissa.

"True," said Rommy. "But maybe something was learned about the value of moderation tonight. That is a good thing to learn."

Leezah read a question for Annissa's team to answer: "Who won the 1971 Australian Grand Prix?"

"What's a grand prix?" asked Annissa.

"It's a car race," replied Aunty Jen.

"Did they have cars in 1971?" asked Annissa. "I didn't think they had cars in the olden days!"

The family continued to play for a while but the game was constantly interrupted by stories and jokes. None of the teams won many coloured chips. Soon Annissa started to yawn. The game was particularly difficult for her as she didn't know the answers to many questions at all. Just before she went up to bed she rolled a three and landed on the green chip square.

Nick asked the question:

"Do mosquitos have teeth?"

Annissa had been bitten by mosquitos many times. She immediately said "Yes!" But before Nick could say whether or not her answer was correct Flip cried, "Wait! Think about it my little tree of life." (Tree of life was Flip's nickname for Annissa because that was what her name meant.) "Do you really think mosquitos bite you with teeth? Or do they sting you?"

Annissa and Rommy thought about it and decided Flip was right.

"No," said Annissa to Nick, "Mosquitos don't have teeth." Finally, Annissa was going to get a question right!

"Wrong!" said Nick. "Mosquitos have teeth!"

"Oh no!" cried Flip.

"Uncle Flip!!!" Annissa chased after Flip with a cushion. The chase ended with Annissa being tickled while Aunty Jen packed the game away.

Nick, Leezah and Annissa hugged and kissed their parents, aunties and uncles 'goodnight' and went upstairs to brush their teeth, read and sleep. Tomorrow the Fitzgeralds would return to Fellowship Farm, and school, and a year's supply of free pineapple!

* * * * *

It was still dark the next morning when the families woke. The Fitzgeralds were used to waking early, but it was very hard for their cousins. When everyone had dressed, packed, eaten breakfast and had morning prayers, they headed out to the cars.

The sun was just rising. Soon they were racing down the freeway. Once again Aunty Jen and Uncle Karim drove over the Harbour Bridge especially for their guests. The sun was rising over the harbour and the water sparkled as if the sun was shining on millions of mirrors. Too quickly the drive over the harbour was over and they continued through the city to the airport.

Aunty Jen and Uncle Karim parked the cars and came in to the airport with the Fitzgerald family. They did not want to waste one minute of the time they could have together. Sydney airport was huge. Olingah, Leezah, and Skye felt they could explore that airport all day and still not see it all.

There were machines at which to check in. There were machines that weighed and took their baggage. And then there was a large section for security. When Rommy had put her handbag on the conveyor belt, they each walked through the arch one by one. When Rommy walked through the arch, it beeped and a red cross appeared. Olingah startled.

Rommy went back and took off her watch, belt and shoes. She put them on the conveyor belt. She walked through the security arch again. Olingah held his breath. "What if Rommy wasn't allowed on the plane?" This time the green light showed.

The rest of the family sat on some nearby chairs and waited while Rommy put her watch, belt and shoes back on. When she had finished they stood up, but before Rommy could join them a woman in a blue uniform stopped her. Olingah's heart missed a beat.

"Open your bag for me please Ma'am," said the woman in the blue uniform. "And stand with your arms out." As Rommy stood there, the woman used a kind of stick to poke in Rommy's bag and touch her arms, legs and back. Olingah wondered what was happening. He thought Rommy was in trouble. "What if they take her away?" he thought. "What if they think she is dangerous?"

The woman slipped something into a machine and waited a moment. Then she nodded at Rommy and said, "Thank you." Rommy picked up her handbag and came over to her family.

Olingah let himself breath again. He hurried toward his mother and wrapped his arms around her. Tears sprung to his eyes. "What were they doing Mummy?" he asked, his voice shaking. Rommy could see Olingah was distressed.

She knelt down so she was at the same height as him. "Darling, nothing. They check lots of passengers. It's just routine. To keep us safer. Look." Rommy was pointing at a passenger who was taking off his belt, and another passenger who had been stopped by the woman in the blue uniform. "It doesn't mean anything bad." She gave her son a big hug.

The family walked down a short flight of stairs and past a big display of lollies and chocolates. The children didn't even want to look at it. They continued past shops selling meals, and then down a long wide hallway with windows. This ended at a gate lounge.

The screen hanging from the ceiling at the gate lounge had the words: GA 960 Launceston 09:15. There were 45 minutes until boarding.

The children played on the travelator nearby, being careful not to cause inconvenience for any other passengers. They pressed their faces against the large windows and watched the planes arriving and leaving, and the workers directing the planes and loading the luggage.

A few minutes before the boarding call, Rommy called the children to the gate lounge. The family gathered for hugs and kisses, tears and farewells, promises to write, and plans to see each other again soon. Then came the call to board. The final kisses were blown and hands waved as the Fitzgerald family disappeared into the carpeted tunnel, and headed for the plane, back to Fellowship Farm.

BOOK FIFTEEN

FLOOD ON FELLOWSHIP FARM

Olingah's fear that something 'bad' might happen, comes true. He wakes one morning to the sound of Skye-Maree screaming the house down.

But with unity, love and patience, the Fitzgerald family's crisis turns into a victory once again, and along the way there is much rain, and much fun.

Falling trees

The Fitzgeralds returned to Fellowship Farm from Sydney, late in the afternoon on Sunday. It rained heavily all the way from Launceston to Kellyton. The dirt road from Kellyton to the farm was covered in water, and in some places rivulets flowed across the road. When they arrived at the farm, Ruha met them on the back veranda with her usual radiant smile. She said that everything had gone well while they were away, but the rain had not stopped falling.

The whole lawn at the back of the house was covered in water. Ruha had moved the puppies' bedding up onto the veranda because she had been worried their dog house would get flooded. Indeed, the dog house now had inches of water on its floor. The Fitzgeralds encouraged Ruha to leave the farm quickly in case the road flooded and her van couldn't get through. She hugged them all goodbye and hurried away.

Inside the farmhouse, the Fitzgeralds added two big logs to the fire burning in the living room, unpacked their suitcase, and made some thick hot vegetable soup for dinner. The children moved the puppies' bedding into the boot room. Even the veranda was no longer providing a dry place for the puppies to sleep, as the wind was blowing the rain under the roof of the veranda.

The children were very grateful that they didn't have to sleep in the boot room! It was fine for the puppies who were tough and used to sleeping outside, but the boot room felt cold and draughty to the children. They hurried inside to have their soup, showers, and prayers, and then they tumbled exhausted into their warm beds.

In the morning, as Flip was getting ready to go out on the farm and the children were preparing for school, the phone rang. It was the principal from Kellyton primary school. She said that a tree had been uprooted from all the rain, and toppled over in the storm. It had damaged several classrooms, so school was cancelled until they could make alternative arrangements. "Yipeee!" cried Skye-Maree. She loved going to school, and she was excited to tell her friends about her weekend in Sydney, but it was fun to have some extra days of weekend too.

"Lucky no one was in the classroom when the tree fell over!" said Olingah, quietly.

"Let us know if there's anything we can do to help," said Flip, and hung up the phone.

The children took off their school uniforms and pulled on some warm home clothes. They set up the Chinese Checkers board in front of the fire, and started to play. Flip kissed them goodbye and went out into the cold rain to check on the farm and its animals. Rommy put on a load of washing, and then started to vacuum the bedrooms. She would leave for the veterinary surgery in Kellyton at lunch time.

After three games of Chinese Checkers, six games of UNO, some drawing, reading, and a game of Monopoly, it was time to pull the washing from the dryer and put it away. Then it was time for lunch. Normally the family shopped at the markets on Sundays, but they had been in Sydney last weekend, so there was not much food in the house. There was some left over soup, and Rommy took a loaf of frozen bread from the freezer to make some toast and butter. Flip didn't come in for lunch as he was too busy on the farm, so when Rommy left for the veterinary surgery the children were at home alone.

As Rommy drove off to work, the cold rain thundered on the roof of the Ute and the farm house. The afternoon sky was dark with thick grey clouds and a strong wind was blowing the branches of the trees.

In the boot room, Flea, Fizz and Flex huddled together in their temporary bed, trying to keep warm and dry. The pigeon cage was covered with a large tarpaulin to protect the birds from the winter weather. But inside the farmhouse, the fire was blazing in the fire place. The children sat on the rug in front of the fire, protected by a fire-screen, surrounded by cardboard, scissors, and balls of coloured wool. They were wrapping wool around cardboard doughnuts.

After some time, Skye-Maree found it hard to push the wool through the hole. She had just about finished. She carefully snipped the wool along the edge of the doughnut. Then tightly tied a piece of wool around the bunch of wool, slipping it between the two pieces of cardboard. When she pulled out the cardboard she was left with a brightly coloured woollen pompom.

Leezah still had some wrapping to do as she was making the biggest pompom. Olingah had just started snipping at his wool. Although he was holding his pompom carefully together, some of the wool in Olingah's had fallen out of place. "Oh no!" he said, when he saw his pompom. Skye-Maree helped him line the wool back up again, finish cutting, and tie the wool between the two pieces of cardboard.

"Thanks Skye," said Olingah. "But it still looks wonky!" he added, with disappointment in his voice.

"Why don't you make another one Olly," said Skye-Maree. "Just make a small one." But Olingah had had enough of making pompoms. He was tired of being inside. Tired of sitting still.

"Let's go have 'boat' races in the rain," suggested Olingah. He was thinking of a game they liked to play: Floating tennis balls on the stream that ran through the farm. It was particularly fun when the stream was full, during a big rain.

"Yeah!" said Leezah and Skye at once.

Leezah quickly finished tying her pompom tightly between the cardboard doughnuts. She pulled out the cardboard and placed her pompom next to Olingah's and Skye's on the mantelpiece.

They worked together to pack up the scissors, bits of cardboard, balls of wool, and little pieces of leftover wool. Leezah threw the cardboard and leftover wool into the fire. The fire flared up briefly as the cardboard caught fire. "Do you want to ask Daddy if we can go play boat races?" Leezah asked Olingah, as she knew he liked to be the one to use the radio.

"Yes please!" Olingah exclaimed, and ran to the kitchen. He picked up the hand held radio with its long grey curly cord, and pressed the button. "Base to mobile one. Over."

Flip was out on the farm, checking that all the animals were safe in the heavy rain.

After a few seconds there was a crackle and Flip's voice said, "Mobile one to base. Over."

"Daddy, can we please go play boat races at the stream in the hill paddock? Over."

"Yes Olly, if you wear your rain gear and stay close together. And please make sure the fire screen is up. Over." It was hard to hear him because of the rain beating on the roof of the Ute.

"Thanks Daddy. Over."

"I just have a couple more paddocks to check and then I'll be home. Over and out."

"Over and out," replied Olingah. After he had hung up the radio, Olingah literally jumped for joy into the living room. "Daddy says we can go! Let's go!"

Ball boats

In an old ice-cream container in the boot room there was a collection of old tennis balls. Some were very old and had no felt left on the outside. Some were green, some yellow, one was pink. They were all dirty. They had been used as balls and as boats by the children, and as toys by the puppies. The children chose a ball each to use as a boat, and they took another three balls – one for each of the puppies.

Dressed in woolly jumpers, tracksuit pants, scarves, beanies, raincoats, rain hats and gumboots, and surrounded by three very excited young dogs, the children waded along the path which had become a stream. Under a tree at the front of the house, Joey stood, sheltering from the rain. When he saw the children leaving the garden and heading up the hill to the paddock behind the farm house, he ventured out into the rain, and followed slowly behind.

Skye-Maree opened the gate to the paddock and let the children, dogs, and wallaby through. She closed the gate carefully behind them. The grass of the paddock by the stream was soggy as they trudged up the hill. The stream itself was gushing down the hill, a swirling brown rush of water leaping over rocks and fallen branches. The puppies struggled in the waterlogged grass, puffing and panting their way up the hill. The puppies had all abandoned their balls at the bottom of the paddock.

When the children reached the top of the paddock, they found a patch of stream that was flowing relatively smoothly. They found a large stick and placed it across the stream. Each of them put their ball behind the stick. The balls bobbed and danced behind the stick, wanting to go with the flow of the water, down the stream. Leezah said, "Ready, set, go!" Skye-Maree lifted the stick and the balls started their journey.

The goal was to be the owner of the ball that first reached the bridge across the stream at the bottom of the paddock. Each child was allowed to rescue a stuck ball once. Other than that they had to rely on the stream itself, or other balls, or even a puppy to give their stuck ball a shove. All the balls started out rushing down the stream.

Olingah's then got caught in an eddy and started swirling around instead of continuing downstream. By chance, Skye's ball landed on top of Olingah's as it reached the same pool, and this gave Olingah's ball the shove it needed to get back into the main current. Skye's ball followed swiftly after. Leezah's ball was racing ahead until it got stuck between a log and a rock. Leezah didn't want to use her one chance to push the ball, so early in the race, so she dropped sticks and rocks into the stream hoping to dislodge her ball.

Leezah found a rock so big that she could hardly lift it, and dropped it into the water near where her ball was stuck. It created a big splash which washed her ball over the log, and down the stream it went. All three of the children were shouting encouragement at their balls, as if the balls were people or animals and could really understand them.

"Come on baldy!" called Skye, "You can catch up with lime-oh! Hurry, hurry, hurry! No, no don't go over there, good ball good ball, yes, THAT'S the way!"

As the balls tumbled down the stream, it looked like Olingah's green ball was going to win. But as his ball floated along a smooth but swift flowing section of the stream, Flex leaped in and grabbed the ball in his mouth. The puppies were nine months old now and the stream, even when full after rain, was not a threat to them. Olingah was not at all worried about Flex. He was, however, not at all pleased that Flex had run off with his ball, just when he was about to win!

Flex clambered out of the stream and stumbled across the soggy paddock with the ball. This was the exact reason the children had given the puppies their own balls! "Fleeeeeex!" shouted Olingah. "You come back here right now!" But Flex thought chasings was a wonderful game to play, and he delighted in having Olingah stagger after him.

Meanwhile Skye's felt-less ball bounced over some rocks on a spout of water and won the race. Skye scooped up the ball just before it went under the bridge. Leezah's ball followed soon after. Olingah chased Flex across the paddock, but eventually gave up and came back to join his sisters at the bridge. When Flex saw the great game of chasings was over, he joined the children at the bridge and dropped the ball in the grass. "You are wicked, evil and naughty," said Olingah to Flex with a grin, giving him a rub between his soaking wet ears. Flex just shook his wet head all over Olingah.

"Shall we go again?" asked Skye-Maree, and everyone nodded vigorously. Olingah picked up the balls they had brought for the puppies and threw them across the paddock. The puppies bounded after them. Meanwhile, the children slogged back up the soggy paddock. At least the rain was starting to ease a little. At the top of the hill, they lined the balls up once again. After Ready! Set! Go! the race was on again.

The children raced down the side of the stream and clambered back up the hill for the rest of the afternoon. They shouted at their balls, and at the puppies, and dropped stones in the river to create waves. Their gumboots filled with water. Their clothes became covered in mud. Their cheeks turned pink and their fingers turned blue. As they had completely lost track of time, they were all surprised to see the orange Ute coming up the main road toward the farm. They suddenly realised that the sun was very close to setting.

The children grabbed their balls and called the puppies. They ran down the muddy slope, through the gate, and over to the farm house. Joey was nowhere to be seen and had probably wandered up to the very top part of the paddock. They arrived just as their mother pulled up. Rommy opened the door of the Ute. She was wearing her vet surgery uniform.

Skye-Maree, giggling, threatened to give her a big muddy hug. Rommy said, "Don't even think about it sister!!" She pulled her gumboots out of the car, pulled her work shoes off, and slipped her gumboots on. she handed some bags of groceries to the children, then slid out of the Ute. The family waded up the path beside the house.

"Where's Daddy?" Rommy asked.

The children realised that Flip had been gone a long time. On the radio he had said he would be home soon.

"He said he was checking a couple more paddocks then coming home," said Olingah.

"I'll radio him, when we get inside," said Rommy. "Please take all your clothes off outside and put them straight into the washing machine! I will run you a spa."

"Thanks Mum!!" the children joyfully exclaimed. A big tub full of warm water and bubbles sounded perfect.

While the children jumped into the spa, which was gradually filling with warm water, Rommy put the washing machine on. She then went into the kitchen and picked up the radio. "Base to mobile one. Over."

There was no reply. Rommy waited a few seconds. Then repeated, "Base to mobile one. Over." Again there was no reply. As she put the groceries away Rommy wondered where Flip might be, now that the sun was setting. If he was away from the Ute he wouldn't hear the radio, and that happened quite often on the farm. But at this time, she thought he would be heading home.

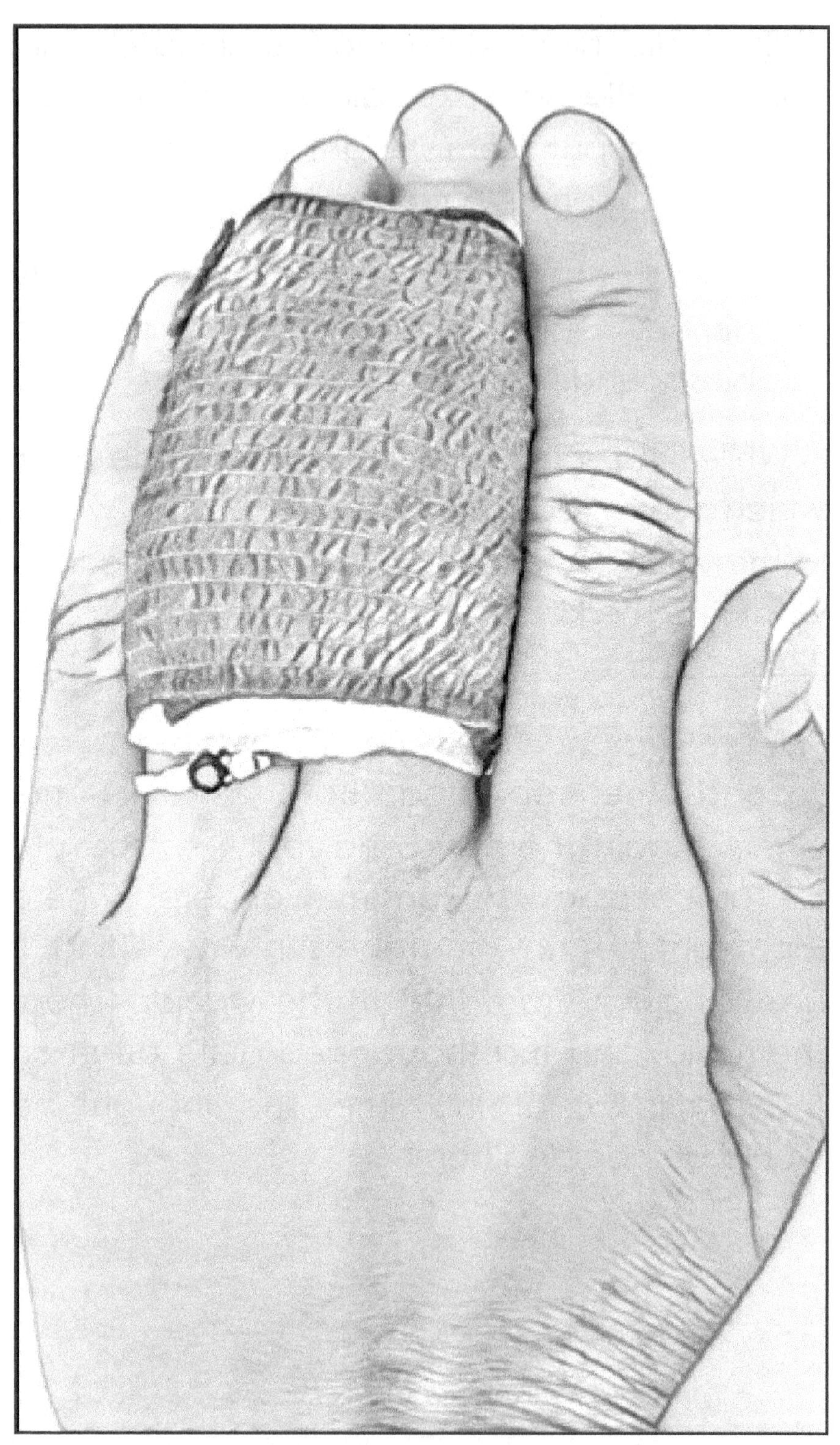

Blood dressing

Rommy changed out of her vet surgery clothes, and into her farm clothes. She had a feeling she might need to go out on the farm, rather than make dinner. She tried again to reach Flip. "Base to mobile one. Over."

Silence.

Rommy went into the bathroom where the children were squirting dirty soapy water at each other with their mouths. "When you children get a deadly disease, don't expect me to visit you in the hospital!" she said sternly with smiling eyes. Then more seriously, she said, "I just want to go and check that all is well on the farm. Will you be okay here by yourselves?"

"Yes Mummy, we can make some cheese toasties and salad for dinner if you like?" replied Leezah. Rommy nodded and smiled.

The rain continued to pour, the air was cold and it was already dark. Rommy drove the Ute up to the shed where the tractor was kept. She grabbed the tow chain and put it behind the driver's seat. The tractor engine started up with a roar. Rommy turned the powerful headlights on, and headed down the slope toward the gate of the farm.

Leezah, Skye-Maree and Olingah played a little longer in the warm water. Then they pulled out the plug, and ran to their own bathroom to get their towels. They dried themselves, and dressed in their warm pyjamas, dressing gowns and ugg boots. They went into the kitchen and opened the fridge. Leezah passed Skye-Maree some bread, cheese, mayonnaise, tomato, cucumber, lettuce, olives, and onion. They took two chopping boards from next to the sink and put them on the kitchen table. Leezah put the bread under the grill to toast. Olingah set the table then went to read his book by the fire.

The girls worked happily together. When the bread was toasted on one side, Leezah took it out and spread a layer of mayonnaise on each slice. She put slices of tomato on top, followed by slices of cheese. She then put everything back under the grill. Skye-Maree was chopping cucumber with a sharp knife, when she heard Olingah start to giggle in the living room. "What's funny Olly?" called Skye.

Olingah started to answer but Skye couldn't hear properly. She turned her head and stretched her neck in the direction of the living room. The knife slid as Skye turned, and instead of slicing the cucumber, Skye sliced her thumb. "Oh no!" said Skye, as blood started to flow onto the chopping board. She hurried over to the sink. Blood flowed into the sink.

"Oh no!" Leezah echoed.

Skye started to wash her bloodied hand under the tap but this seemed to make the blood flow even faster.

"I'll ask Mum what to do," said Leezah quickly, and reached for the radio.

"Base to mobile three. Over," said Leezah, her heart racing as blood streamed down the sink with the water from the tap.

Mobile meant vehicle. The white Ute was mobile one. The orange Ute was mobile two. The tractor was mobile three.

"Mobile three to base," came the faint reply accompanied by the sound of rain thundering on the roof of the tractor.

"Mummy. Skye. Has. Cut. Her. Hand. What. Should. I. Do. Over," said Leezah loudly, slowly, and clearly.

There was a lot of crackling and the rain was almost deafening. Then Rommy's voice came through: "Wrap (shhhh) firmly (shhhh) clean (crackle crackle shhhhh) dry tea towel, (shhhh) pressure (crackle shhhh crackle) above the heart (shhh). Over."

Leezah didn't waste any time. "Thanks-over-and-out," she replied, and hurried to hook the radio back in its place. She grabbed a tea towel from the kitchen drawer and wrapped Skye's thumb in it. She told Skye to press firmly on the place where it was cut, and Skye lifted it above shoulder level.

Skye-Maree often caused herself injuries one way or another – often through the sport she loved to play. She was used to having cuts and bruises, so she wasn't too worried about her hand. But she was grateful that Leezah was taking care of her.

"Thank you nurse Leezah," she said, as she sat down at the kitchen table, keeping her hands above her shoulder.

Leezah rinsed the blood from the chopping board, and from the cucumber. "Salad with Skye-blood, yuck!" she said. It was then that Leezah noticed the smell of smoke.

"The toasties!" both Leezah and Skye cried at once. Leezah pulled the grill out. The edges of the toast were black and some of the cheese had gone from softly melted to dry, and dark yellow or black.

"Oh no!" the girls groaned together.

Leezah turned off the grill and opened the kitchen door. The cold winter air rushed into the kitchen, clearing the smoke, but chilling the girls. As soon as the smoke had cleared, Leezah hurried to shut the door.

"What should I do?" she asked her sister. "Mummy and Daddy are going to be very hungry when they get home. All we have is burnt toasties and half a salad with blood dressing!" The girls started to giggle.

The burnt toasties were very hot. One by one Leezah carefully pulled the charred sandwiches out of the grill and piled them onto a large plate. Her finger tips burned as she pulled each piece of bread out by its edges. When all ten pieces of bread and cheese were on the plate she took it outside. Standing on the veranda, she gave a whistle. Flea, Flex and Fizz scampered along the veranda. Leezah dropped the burnt toasties in front of them. The puppies were very happy to serve as compost bins. But their little noses and tongues found the burnt toasties too hot to eat. They danced around the unexpected supper, until the cold winter air cooled the hot grilled cheese. Within seconds of them cooling, the dogs had wolfed them down. Leezah went back inside and started the process again. This time without a helper.

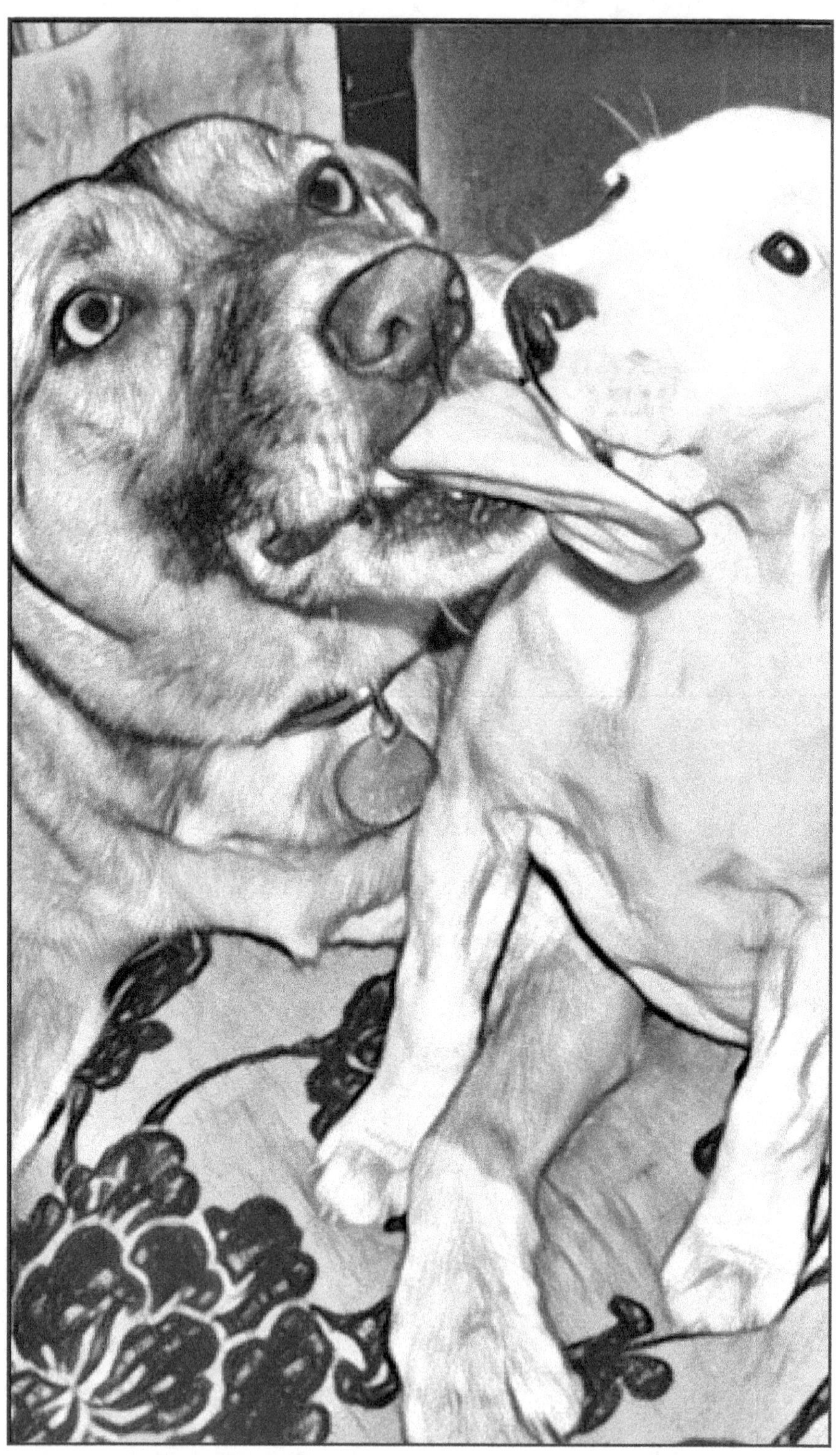

Loving licks

Half an hour later, the table was set and the toasties and salad were on large plates in the middle of the table. Leezah started to wonder where her parents could be. She went to the front of the house and pressed her face against the sunroom window, peering out into the night. The thick curtain of rain made everything outside dark.

Beyond the rain, heavy clouds covered all the stars and the moon. In addition to this, the road from Kellyton out to the farms had no street lights. Leezah peered through the rain for any glimmer of headlights from the Ute or tractor, but there was nothing.

Leezah walked back to the kitchen and picked up the two-way radio. "Base to mobile one, over." Leezah listened hard for a voice or even a crackle.

Silence.

"Base to mobile three, over." Leezah held her breath so as not to miss a single sound.

Silence.

She looked at the red plastic clock on the kitchen wall. Seven o'clock.

Leezah walked into the living room. Olingah and Skye-Maree were reading on the couch in front of the fire.

"I'm starving!" said Olingah.

"Where are Mum and Dad?" asked Skye.

"I don't know where they are," said Leezah. "Maybe we should have some dinner and they can eat when they get home?"

Olingah strongly agreed. He dropped his book on the couch and hurried to wash his hands and sit up at the table. Skye-Maree and Leezah joined him.

"May we eat this food with thanks, and use its energy to help all beings live together in peace, love, joy, and harmony," they prayed together.

Olingah felt so hungry, he thought he could eat all the toasties by himself, but after one toastie and some salad his tummy was full. Soon after, he started to feel very sleepy. He took his plate to the kitchen and went to brush his teeth. After all the running in the rain, and then the long wait for dinner, Skye was also sleepy. She followed her brother, and by quarter to eight, the children were sitting in front of the fire singing their evening prayers.

"Please make Mummy and Daddy come home soon," prayed Olingah, with all his heart. "Please don't let them be hurt. Please keep all the animals safe in the rain."

Leezah remembered the conversation they had had with Rommy and Flip in the car on the way to the airport.

"Please give us strength to deal with whatever happens," Leezah prayed. Then she started to sing, "Rely upon God. Trust in Him. Praise Him, and call Him continually to mind. He verily turneth trouble into ease, and sorrow into solace, and toil into utter peace. He verily hath dominion over all things."

After prayers, Olingah and Skye-Maree went off to bed. "Wake me up when Mummy and Daddy get home," Skye requested. Leezah nodded and told them she would come in to the bedroom soon. She went back to the kitchen and picked up the two-way radio. She whispered a prayer, then she said, "Base to mobile one, over."

Silence.

"Base to mobile one, over."

Not even a scratch or a crackle. No sound of rain on the Ute roof. No shoshing of a radio just out of range.

"Base to mobile three, over." Leezah tried to reach her mother in the tractor.

No response.

"Base to mobile three, over." Leezah tried again.

Nothing.

The children were rarely home alone, and they had never been alone at night before. Leezah wondered if she should call someone, maybe even the police. She wondered if her parents were just out of range, or couldn't hear the radio. She wondered if they would be home soon, or if they were stuck somewhere, or even worse, hurt. Leezah didn't know what she should do.

She went outside to get a log for the fire from the room between the boot room and the outside toilet. The puppies heard her open the kitchen door and came scampering out of the boot room. They slipped and slid on the slippery wet veranda. Leezah squatted down and stroked their soft warm bodies. They clambered onto her bent knees, licked her hands and tried to lick her face. Their little doggy kisses and wagging tails made Leezah feel comforted, and more worried at the same time. She started to cry.

The puppies licked her tears and she snuggled them for a few minutes. When she could no longer stand to be out in the winter air without a coat, she rubbed their heads one last time. She shooed the puppies back into the dry boot room, grabbed a log of wood, and went inside. She pulled back the fire-screen and put the log carefully onto the fire. The hot coals soon set the strings of bark alight, and the flames flared up. Leezah sat by the fire. She turned her heart toward 'Abdu'l-Bahá and prayed all the prayers she knew, one after the other.

When she finished, Leezah felt a deep peace. She knew that whatever might happen, Bahá'u'lláh would give them all the strength they would need. Leezah also felt very sleepy. She lay down on the couch by the fire and fell fast asleep. Outside, the rain fell harder and harder on Fellowship Farm.

Leezah dreamt that she was walking through falling snow. Her skin was cold and her teeth were chattering. She was trying to see through the snow. She needed to find something important. She couldn't work out which way to go. Then she heard someone calling her name: "Leezah. Leezah."

"I can't stop," said Leezah. "I have to keep looking."

"Leezah. Leezah," the gentle voice came again and Leezah felt a hand on her arm, coming through the snow. Slowly Leezah opened her eyes. The fire was out. The room was cold. There was in fact a hand on her arm. It was Rommy's.

Leezah was muddled by sleep and confused. She felt happy and sad and scared and relieved. She started to cry. Rommy wrapped her arms around her daughter and drew her close in a big hug. Flip came and knelt by the couch and wrapped his arms around both of them. Soon Leezah's confusion, fear and sadness passed and she felt flooded with relief. But this just made her cry even harder!

"Where were you?" she asked as her tears subsided. "What happened?"

"We were on the farm," replied Rommy quietly. "We've never had so much rain at once. Tomorrow we might even have to think about what we will need to do if the river overflows." Then, when they had finished hugging, Rommy suggested: "Why don't you go to bed now darling? We'll tell you everything in the morning. It's past midnight now." Leezah nodded and Flip led her to her bed and helped her up the ladder to the top bunk.

But when the morning came there would be no time for stories for the Fitzgeralds of Fellowship Farm.

Breakfast in the barn

"Muuuuuuuuum!!!!," screamed Skye-Maree. "Daaaaaddddyyyyy!!"

Her screams woke Olingah, Leezah, Rommy and Flip from their sleep. The house was still dark, as the sun would not rise for more than an hour. When Skye-Maree had woken in her dark bedroom, she had stepped out of her bed, and straight into water almost up to her knee. The bedroom was like a lake. Rommy and Flip came splashing up the hall and into the bedroom in their pyjamas. Skye-Maree and Olingah were now crying and Leezah, just waking on the top bunk, was trying to work out what was going on.

"It's ok," said Flip calmly but quickly. "The house is flooded. Grab some warm clothes from your cupboard and come out to the veranda." None of the lights were working so the children fumbled around in the dark and headed out to the veranda. As they walked through the kitchen, Rommy was throwing food into a carry bag and Flip was filling bottles with water. There were sleeping bags on the kitchen table, and Flip asked the children to carry them out to the boot room.

In the boot room everyone put on their wet weather gear. They pulled on their gumboots, even though the water at the side of the house was deeper than their boots. At least with their boots on they wouldn't step on anything sharp under the water. "We will need to head up to the haybarn," said Rommy, "to be safe from the flood waters."

"What about the puppies?" cried Leezah. Nobody had free arms to carry three large excited dogs.

"They can swim down the side of the house," said Rommy and then walk with us up the hill. "Call them to follow us."

The family started to wade down the path beside the house. The water quickly filled their gumboots and soaked their pyjamas. "Flea! Flex! Fizz!" the children's high pitched voices called frantically. The puppies plopped off the steps of the veranda into the flooded garden. They swam quickly after the children.

"Lucky Joey stayed in the hill paddock after we played boat races!" said Olingah. The front garden was a lake.

After they had waded through the front gate and partway up the hill toward the barn, the Fitzgeralds took off their gumboots and tipped out litres of icy water. As they passed the hen house, which was just above the level of the water, Flip opened the hen house door and the gate to their pen. "They need to be free to go anywhere on the farm, to keep safe," said Flip. "The water may rise further."

As the family and puppies climbed up the hill, they peered through the dark morning and back over the house, garden, and road. Everything was submerged in a dark lake of water. There was no way any car could travel down the road. The road was completely invisible. Half of the fences were under water too. The family hurried up the hill.

It was a huge relief to be out of the pouring rain as they stepped into the shelter of the haybarn. The farm dogs in the tractor shed next door barked excitedly. Flip ducked next door and threw them a bone from the fridge in the shed.

Rommy turned on a torch and shone it on the bales of hay stacked half way up the tall wall of the barn. The children and Flip clambered up the bales. The children had spent many happy hours playing on top of the hay and they were quick to climb to the top. Many helping hands pushed and pulled three fat dogs up the hay bales to the dusty dry space at the top. Rommy followed.

Flip spread out a couple of sleeping bags. "Wet pyjama pants off," he said. The children didn't need to be told! They were soaked and freezing. All five pulled off their wet pyjamas and flung them off to the side. Then they pulled on the clothes they had brought from their cupboards – warm socks, fleecy tracksuit pants, woolly jumpers, hats and mittens. Sitting on the sleeping bags, Rommy and Flip wrapped the other sleeping bags around the shoulders of the children. They started to prepare breakfast.

"Now, who wants porridge?" asked Flip, "and who wants toast? I'll have a nice cup of tea please," he added.

"How about untoasted bread, cold cheese, apple, banana, and cold water instead?"

suggested Rommy, laying out those exact items.

"Perfect," nodded Flip with a wink. "Received most gratefully."

Everyone was hungry – especially Flip and Rommy. As the sun started to rise, hidden by thick clouds and pouring rain, all the food spread for breakfast disappeared into grateful tummies.

"What happened last night?" asked Leezah. "Where were you?"

Flip started to explain.

When the children had radioed him to ask permission to go to the creek, Flip was planning to check the cows in the river paddock and then head home. He knew that Rommy was at the surgery and he didn't want the children to be alone too long. But in the river paddock he found that a cow had slipped into a small gully and under a log, and was stuck.

The cow was very scared and the log was very heavy. It took Flip a long time to free the cow. When he finished, he checked that the cow was not injured. Luckily she was okay.

By then the sun had set. Flip went to get back in the Ute and head home. He then discovered that while he had been cutting the log, and digging away at the mud, to free the cow, the Ute had sunk in the rain-soaked paddock, and was bogged. He tried to get the Ute out of the bog by laying pieces of wood under and in front of the wheels. That's why he had missed the radio calls. But the Ute was too bogged.

He was just about to radio for help, when Rommy turned up with the tractor. With the tractor, Rommy helped pull the Ute out of the mud and towed it to the gravel road that runs through the paddock. It was then they noticed the river water was starting to overflow the banks, just a little.

They spent several hours in the dark and rain, herding the cows in the river paddock across the road and up the hill to higher ground. It was very boggy and the cows could not move quickly. As the pigsty was also in a low-lying part of the paddock they also had to move the pigs to higher ground. It was after midnight when they finished and came home. Flip had not eaten since breakfast and Rommy had not eaten since lunchtime. They were very hungry, very cold, wet, muddy and tired. They had showers and collapsed into bed, until they were woken by Skye's screams and found the house had turned into a boat!

"I was so worried Mummy!" said Leezah, remembering the fear of the evening before. "I'm so glad you're safe."

"So am I," said Rommy. "We are very lucky, and we are lucky that we live in such safety nearly all the time."

"I was listening to a young man on the radio last week," said Flip, "who lives in Iraq."

"That's where Bahá'u'lláh lived!" said Skye-Maree.

"Yes, it is," said Flip, "but now it is a place with a lot of conflict and violence. The young man on the radio said that each time one of the family leaves the house – to go to school, or to the market to buy food – they don't know if that person will come back safely, or be killed by a gun or a bomb."

Leezah was shocked by what her father told her.

"Imagine," she said, "if every time you went out on the farm, or we went to school, or to the Kellyton markets, we didn't know whether we would get blown up or make it back home!"

"You know what!" said Olingah, "We still haven't had our spiritual breakfast! So let's have some prayers for the people in Iraq and for the cows on Fellowship Farm!"

"Good idea Olly," said Rommy.

Monsters in the tunnels

As the sun rose dimly over the flooded farm, the Fitzgeralds sat reverently in the dusty hay barn, grateful that they were dry and safe, and praying that everyone in the world could be safe too. They sat for a minute in silent meditation.

"What are we going to do Mum?" asked Skye-Maree, when they had all finished. "How long are we going to stay in the barn?" Skye-Maree had a full belly. She was with her favourite people in the world, and with her beloved dogs – who were very happy to be with their beloved people. She was snug and warm in her winter clothes and wrapped in a sleeping bag. She loved the hay barn and knew they could play happily there all day if they had to. So, it was all feeling like a happy adventure and Skye-Maree thought it wouldn't be too bad to stay there all week!

Flip was not in the habit of carrying a mobile phone. He had had a few, but he kept dropping them in the mud or leaving them around the farm. So he depended on the two-way radio for communication. Rommy had a mobile phone but the battery was dead, as she had not put it on to charge when she got home late last night. And the reception from the farm was often very poor anyway. So there was no way to call anyone.

The rain was still falling and when they looked out the window in the side of the barn, they could see the water was still slowly rising. The chickens had left their pen and found their way up the hill and into the haybarn. The family could hear them scratching around in the loose hay below, gently bock-bock-bocking.

"Well, we have enough food and water for one or two more meals," replied Rommy. "The other farms along the river will be flooded too. I guess the emergency services will send people out to the farms to see if anyone needs help."

"Until then, I guess we just wait patiently,' added Flip.

Spending a few hours – or even a whole day, playing in the hay, did not require any patience for Leezah, Skye-Maree and Olingah! They immediately began to shuffle the bales around to make a small tunnel going down into the stack and then out the side. Rommy and Flip wrapped themselves in the abandoned sleeping bags. They settled back on the hay to catch up on some of the sleep they had missed the night before.

The sun struggled higher into the sky bringing a little more light to the barn, but no extra heat! The rain pounded on and on, beating on the corrugated iron roof of the shed like a non-stop drum. The sweet smell of the hay brought happy memories of cutting and baling the hay in summer, and feeding the cows in winter. The children squeezed themselves between the bales, using their bodies to widen the tunnel. Leezah went first.

Halfway down she suddenly felt like she was getting stuck. She was upside down in a tiny tunnel of hay and she felt she couldn't move forward or backward. She started to feel panicky. Skye saw that she had stopped moving forward. She grabbed hold of the bottom of Leezah's feet which were just poking out the top of the hole. She gave her sister a big push. Leezah slithered forward and out the hole in the side of the pile of bales. She slithered down the side of the stack of hay, landing hands first on the hay-covered floor of the barn.

Leezah's hair, clothes, socks were covered in sticks of hay: yellow, green and brown; short and long. Her face was dusty and scratched. But she was grinning from ear to ear. She looked up to see the heads of Flea, Flex and Fizz hanging over the edge of the cliff of hay. Their pink tongues were hanging out and their heads wiggled from side to side.

As Leezah looked up, Skye-Maree came slithering down. Leezah had helped widen the hole, so Skye didn't get so stuck. She slid straight down and then out to the side. Soon she also looked like a hay monster, as she plopped down beside her sister.

Olingah, who was smaller than the girls, came whizzing through on the slippery hay and tumbled out the hole at the side. His sisters grabbed him as he popped out so that he wouldn't hurt himself dropping headfirst on to the floor. Then it was time to climb back up and do it all again.

As they were climbing back up they heard a yelp. Then someone else appeared at the hole in the side of the haystack. It was Flea!

She had slithered down the tunnel. She stood, perched on the edge of the hole, peering out, with her pink tongue dusty and covered in dry grass.

"Look! There's Flea!" cried Skye-Maree. The children started to laugh and climbed back down. Together the three of them helped Flea safely to the floor.

"Now we need to help her get back up!" said Olingah. For seven-year-old Olingah the nearly fully grown dogs were very heavy.

"Let's leave her down here, and see if she finds her own way up," suggested Leezah.

The children clambered up. Fizz and Flex greeted them at the top with licks and wags. Rommy and Flip were fast asleep so the children called softly, "Flea, come on Flea, here Flea, Flea-Flea." They hung their heads over the side of the hay.

Flea looked up at them high above her. She tried to climb straight up the cliff of hay, with no success. The children kept calling her softly. Olingah walked over to the other side of the barn and Flea followed him with her eyes. Then she scampered over to that side. The bales were in a more jagged formation on that side of the barn and Flea found a way to clamber up. It was climbing up the side of a pyramid. Flea was very excited when she made it to the top and Olingah gave her a big cuddle.

Olingah and Flea trotted back over the top hay bales to the tunnel. This time Skye-Maree went first and Flea went second! Followed by Olingah, Fizz, Flex and then Leezah. One by one they slithered down the tunnel, out the hole and down onto the floor. The dogs found that they could also manage the drop from the hole to the floor without help. When they had all slithered down and out, the puppies and children ran over to the side of the barn where the bales were sticking out. All six of them clambered back up.

After almost an hour of slithering, running, climbing, slithering, running, climbing, the children decided to add some more parts to their tunnel. By pushing the bales and forcing their bodies between them, they extended the tunnel and added a new one. They were having so much fun, that the hours passed quickly.

YAMAHA

Floating along the road

Late in the morning Rommy and Flip woke from their nap. They folded the sleeping bags and came over to where the children were playing. "Come down the tunnel Daddy!" cried Olingah excitedly.

"I'm not allowed," said Flip.

"Why not?" asked Olingah.

"Can't you read the sign?" said Flip pointing to the air above the tunnel.

"What does the sign say?" asked Skye-Maree. She knew there was no point in saying that there was no sign.

"It says: 'Strictly hay-monsters only.'"

"Anyone want some lunch?" asked Rommy.

"No no no! Can't you see the other sign?" asked Flip.

"What does the other sign say Daddy?" asked Skye-Maree.

"It says 'DO NOT FEED THE HAY MONSTERS' in three languages," replied Flip.

"I'll take the risk," said Rommy.

Flip and Rommy laid out the sleeping bags which had already served as a table, couches and as beds. They started to put out some bread and honey and peanut butter.

While lunch was being 'served' Olingah wandered around the top of the haybarn, peering out each of the dirty windows. The windows were dusty and covered in cobwebs and it was hard to see anything through them. But when he got to the windows at the front of the barn, he saw something orange that made him call out.

"Mummy! Daddy! Leezah! Skye! Come and see!"

Leezah and Skye-Maree ran over to the window, with Flea, Flex and Fizz following closely behind. Through the glass thick with years of dust, they could see the house and farm under a layer of water. It was strange to see their home standing in the middle of a brown lake. Half the front gate was hidden by water. Along what-used-to-be the road, came a bright orange boat with a motor on the back. In the boat were two people wearing bright green jackets.

"There's a boat coming!" cried Leezah.

Rommy and Flip immediately left the lunch preparation. They didn't even stop to look out the window. They slid down the front of the hay stack, pulled their wet weather gear on, and hurried out into the rain. They jogged down the hill toward the house until they were standing on the edge of the flood waters. They waved their arms above their heads. As the children watched from the top of the barn, the people in green jackets waved back.

The children slithered down the haystack and hurried to put their wet weather gear on. Their gumboots were still soaking wet, and they were icy cold. The children ran down the hill to wait with their parents. The people in the boat had arrived at the gate, which was wide open as usual. They drove the boat through. As they got close to where the Fitzgerald family was waiting, they turned off the engine and pulled up the motor.

The boat drifted toward the edge. The people in green jackets stepped out of the boat, and held onto it by a strong rope. They were smiling, and were delighted to see the family smiling warmly back.

"Wet enough for you?" said the man, with a strong accent. "Did someone leave the plug in the bath and the bath taps on?" he asked the children.

"Skye did it," Leezah answered, pointing at Skye-Maree.

"Och Skye," he said. "We can't be cross with you for too long. You've got the same name as my home! I come from the island of Skye!" Skye-Maree's eyebrows shot up, under her woolly hat and raincoat. She gave the man from Skye a big grin.

The other person from the boat was a woman. "Hi, I'm Louisa," she said. "And this is Colby." Louisa pointed at the man from Skye. "We're going to take you somewhere safe and dry til the floods subside. Are there any animals on the farm that you are concerned about?"

"The horses, pigs, and cows are up the top of the hill paddock," said Rommy.

"And so is Joey!' said Olingah.

"And the chickens are free."

"And there are the puppies," said Olingah.

"Yes, I see that," said Louisa, squatting down to give Flex a rub between the ears. In thanks, Flex shook her head and body all over Louisa. Louisa's wet weather gear was already very wet so it didn't make much difference. "The puppies can come with us to the shelter. There are a lot of people from Kellyton who needed to bring pets so we have made it a pet-friendly shelter."

"There are some caged pigeons behind the house," added Flip. "Their cage is high off the ground but perhaps we should open the door of the cage so they can get out if they need to. And I'll just let the farm dogs off their chains and lock them in the tractor shed with plenty of water and food."

Flip went back up the hill to the tractor shed to attend to the farm dogs. He took several meaty bones out of the old shed fridge and filled three big buckets with water. The dogs were very happy to be off their chains and to have lots of food. Flip slipped out and shut the shed door behind him. He pulled the beam of wood across the front of the doors to secure them. Then he trotted back down the hill.

Louisa and Colby handed each person a bright orange life jacket. They were bulky and it was hard to fit them over the wet weather gear. They buckled at the front with black plastic clips. Leezah felt like she was going to suffocate, but she knew she had to wear it!

Colby and Louisa directed Rommy and Flip to get into the boat first. "So you can help the children and the dogs get in safely," Colby explained. With the help of Louisa and Colby on the shore, they managed to get the dogs into the boat. At first the dogs were very excited and ran from one side of the boat to the other. "Sit!" shouted Flip sternly. The three dogs immediately settled, moved to one end of the boat, and sat. "Otherwise you're going to tip us all into the water," Flip added. When the dogs were settled, Louisa and Colby helped the children get into the boat without getting more water in their gumboots. One by one they lifted the children, up, over the shallow water and into the bright orange canvas boat. Flip and Rommy helped them into the boat. One by one they adjusted to being on a gently rocking surface, and found a place to sit.

Louisa pushed the boat away from the soggy grass. She lowered the motor, and started it. She steered the boat slowly toward the house. It felt very strange to be floating across their driveway! When they got to the front gate, Colby asked the Fitzgeralds to stay in the boat. He had special gumboots all the way up to his chest, that protected him from getting wet. He climbed out of the boat, and waded through the deep water beside the house. He crossed the back lawn which had turned into a deep pond, and opened the door of the pigeon cage. The pigeons were perched together on the top rail. The water had not reached the bottom of their pen due to the long poles on which it sat. But the dog house was almost completely submerged!

Colby waded back down the side of the house and skilfully climbed back into the boat without tipping it over. They then floated away from the house and out through their front gate. The children thought it wonderful fun to be having a boat ride. It reminded them of going fishing with Uncle Jack, when he visited. And it was especially fun to be boating down the road! As they went along there was a break in the rain. The sky was still grey and dark, but the rain stopped falling for a while.

"Have you been to the Hendersons' farm?" asked Leezah as they cruised past the Hendersons' front gate.

"Aye," replied Colby. "you're the last from the farms. There isn't anyone on any of the properties between the coast and Kellyton any more, as far as we know."

"I hope the flood didn't give Mr Henderson another heart attack."

"He seemed to be okay," said Colby, "If you're talking about the gentleman who lives in the farm to the left here."

Leezah nodded.

"Where are we going?" she asked.

"And how long will we stay there?" asked Olingah.

"And what's going to happen to our house?" asked Skye.

"Yes, and the animals on the farm?" Olingah enquired.

Puggle protector

"I can only answer the first of those questions," smiled Colby. "We are going to the shelter that's been set up by the Red Cross on the grounds of Limedale High School."

No one could really answer the other questions, so they just had to wait and see. As they motored along, Olingah started to wonder about the wombats and echidnas, rabbits and frill-necked lizards. Where did they go when the water started to rise? Sometimes when they were driving along the road to the farm they would see those animals crawling through the grass on the side of the road.

"Did the water rise quickly Daddy?" he asked.

"Probably quite quickly," Flip replied.

"Do you think the wombats and the echidnas had time to get away?"

"Well, most of them would have, but maybe not all of them," Flip answered honestly. "Echidnas can dive under water and swim, so if they got caught by surprise they could try to swim toward land. And wombats can run as fast as an Olympic sprinter if they need to, so if they ran in the right direction, they could definitely get away from the rising waters."

Olingah was happy to hear that. "Are there any baby echidnas or wombats at this time of year?"

"Well, yes, this is the time of year for puggles."

"Puggles??" laughed Olingah.

"That's what baby echidnas are called Olly," grinned Flip.

"No they're not!" said Olingah, but he looked at his mother to see what Rommy said.

Rommy nodded. "Even though it sounds like Mr. Make-up-words here just made it up, baby echidnas are actually called puggles. And baby wombats are called joeys.'

"Wombats have joeys at all times of year, so there probably would have been some affected by the flood, unfortunately."

Olingah felt very sad at the thought of puggles and joeys drowning. He wished he could have saved them. He imagined himself with a snorkel and goggles, swimming through the flood waters.

He would call out in their language and they would call back. He would find the burrows and carry all the echidnas, wombats, puggles and joeys to dry land. He would take them up to the bushland at the top of the hill paddock. They would all dig new burrows and be safe and dry.

These thoughts made Olingah feel very happy. He was so lost in his imagination, that it was a shock for him to see that the boat had motored all the way through Kellyton and was now pulling up at a place where the road started to climb a hill, leading out of the town.

There were other small orange boats dropping people at the same place, and a big bus was parked about 50 metres away from the water's edge. Skye-Maree saw her friend, Zoe and Zoe's big sister Meiya, standing on the road. They were with their parents, and their pets. Skye smiled and waved.

Before Flea, Flex, and Fizz were helped out of the boat Colby took three leashes out of a box of supplies and clipped them onto the dogs' collars. Leezah asked what else was in the box of supplies.

"This is like a magic box!" said Colby. "Whatever we need, we have! Leashes, collars, dog food, boxes for cats, people food, baby formula, water, bandages, Panadol, woolly socks, blankets, hats, asthma puffers, chocolate, even toys! You were our easiest customers. You didn't need anything except some leashes."

The family climbed out of the boat with help from Louisa and Colby. As soon as their feet touched the ground, Flea Flex and Fizz were straining at the leashes. They wanted to go and talk to the other dogs. It was very rare that they had contact with other pet dogs and they looked as excited as if they were going to a party.

"Flea heel!" said Olingah as his arm nearly got yanked out of his shoulder.

"Fizz heel!" growled Leezah.

"Flex heel!" followed Skye-Maree sternly.

When the dogs had settled down, the children turned back to Louisa and Colby.

"Thank you very much for rescuing us from the farm," said Leezah, speaking for all of them.

"You are most welcome."

"Will we see you again?" asked Flip.

"Yes," said Colby. "We will be helping at the shelter, once all the residents of Kellyton are brought to safety. See you later!"

Skye-Maree walked Flex over to where Zoe was standing next to her mother. Skye-Maree could see that Zoe's mother was crying. Zoe also looked very sad. Skye gave Zoe a big hug.

"Hullo Mrs Fischer," she said to Zoe's mother. Zoe's mother just gave a little wave hello. But she didn't speak.

"What's wrong?" whispered Skye-Maree to Zoe. "Did something bad happen?"

Zoe's eyes grew wide, and then her brow furrowed. "Are you crazy?" she asked her friend.

Skye-Maree didn't know what to say. "A bit," she said.

"The whole town is flooded der brain!" said Zoe.

"Oh," said Skye, "I know! It was so scary when I woke up in a lake! But then we had a picnic breakfast in the hay barn and got to play in the hay, and then we had a ride in the boat, and now we get to have a sleepover with Flea, Flex, Fizz and you!"

"Mum's really upset about all the furniture getting wrecked, and both our cars are under water! We don't know when we can go back home. And this morning we had eels swimming through our kitchen!" said Zoe.

"Yuk!!" replied Skye-Maree, wrinkling her nose.

Just then Skye-Maree heard a loud 'glock'. It was the sound Flip made with his tongue when he was calling the children. She waved goodbye to her friend and hurried over to her family.

Everyone was being encouraged to board the bus as it was leaving for Limedale. As the families from Kellyton and surrounding farms, climbed onto the bus, two men in bright green jackets gave each of them a paper bag.

When they had all found seats, and settled the dogs on the floor, the children opened the paper bags. Inside each bag was a cheese, tomato and lettuce sandwich, an apple, a chocolate bar, a box of juice, a napkin and a bag of peanuts. The children were ravenous. Olingah was especially excited about the chocolate bar. He ate that first, just to make sure he didn't miss out.

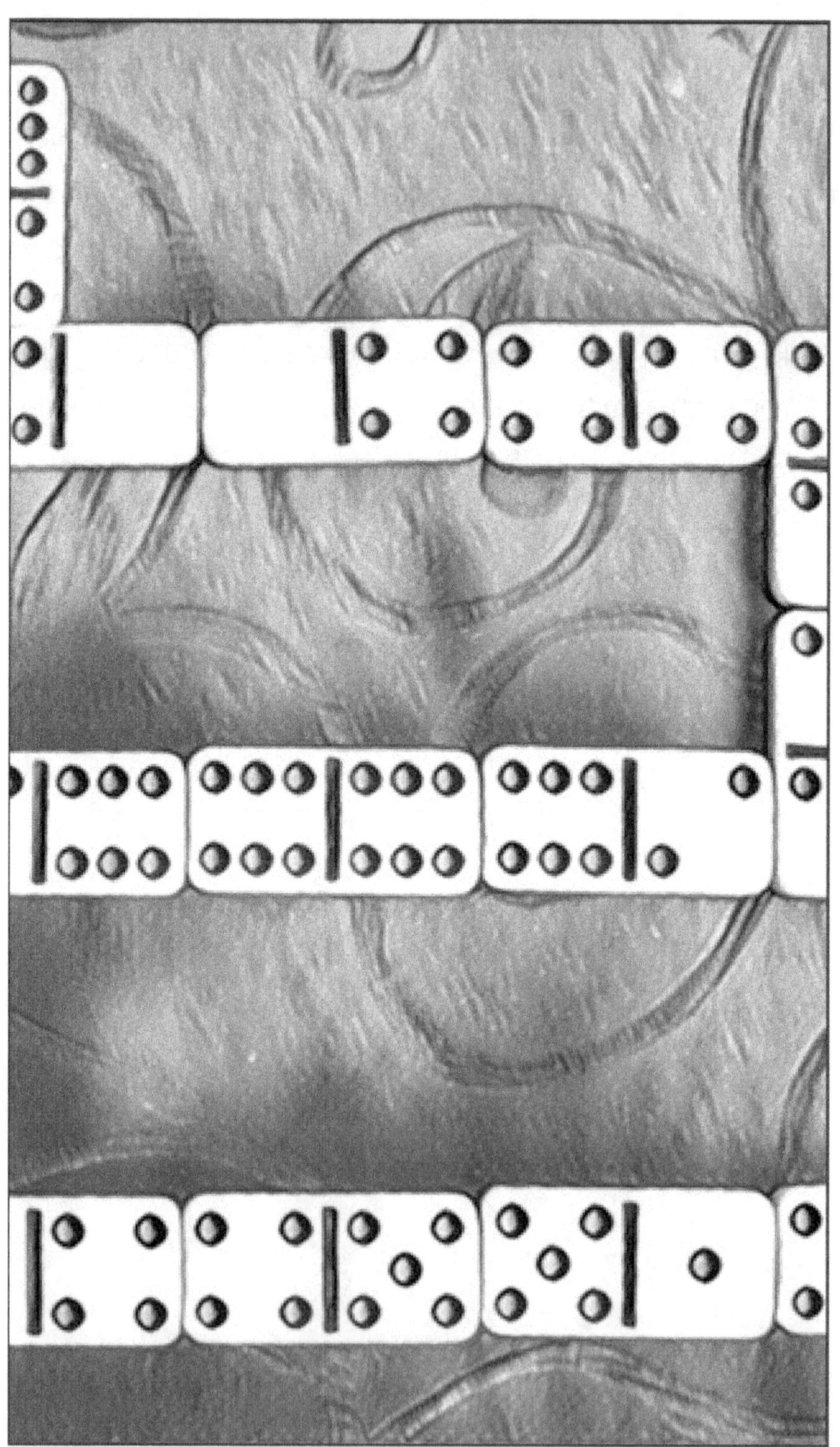

Wonderful wee bairns

It took about half an hour to get to Limedale on the bus. Luckily for Skye-Maree the road wasn't very windy, and the trip was short, so she didn't get too car-sick. As they drove along, the children looked out the windows. None of the farms they passed were as flooded as where they had come from, but other parts of the countryside were very wet.

The creeks and rivers had become torrents of rushing gushing brown foamy water carrying branches and other debris downstream to the sea. The water in one of the rivers was nearly as high as the bridge itself. The paddocks looked like rice paddies, with a layer of water across them. The ducks and other birds were having a wonderful time in their new playgrounds. And as the bus drove along the road the big wheels splashed through huge puddles, spraying fountains of water up the side of the bus. But the rain was no longer falling.

When they arrived at the high school which had been turned into a shelter, the families were led from the bus into the entrance of a large gymnasium. They were taken to a registration table to register. Each of them wrote their name, date of birth and address on a large piece of paper. Even the names of Flea, Flex and Fizz were registered. There were some questions about the dogs, like whether they had had their vaccinations, whether they were desexed.

When all the questions were answered, the children were shown to the outside basketball court, which had been set up to house most of the dogs. Flea, Flex, and Fizz were ecstatic. They dashed off as soon as they were let off their leashes. So many new friends to make!

The family was then led back past the registration table and into the gym. There were rows of mattresses lining the floor. The mattresses were made up into beds, with pillows, sheets and blankets. Some of the 'beds' had belongings or people on them. Others were empty. The hall was full of people from Kellyton. It felt like they were at the Kellyton Sunday market! A woman in a bright green jacket led the Fitzgeralds to a group of five empty beds on one side of the hall. There was a power point with a power board plugged into it. There were already some mobile phones plugged in to it.

"You can plug your phone in here if you need to," said the guide. "But be careful. You can't trust everyone at a shelter. You should keep an eye on your belongings."

"I don't have my charger with me," said Rommy.

"There are spare chargers over there," the woman pointed to a box of leads. Rommy hurried to borrow one. She returned to the beds and plugged her phone in straight away.

They were then shown to a room that normally served as the year seven classroom. The room was full of clothes and shoes that had been donated. There were long racks and huge piles of clothes, sorted roughly by size. The woman who was guiding them told them to take whatever they needed for the next few days.

There were many other people looking through the clothes for things that fit. The first priority for Leezah, Skye-Maree and Olingah was to find something to replace the wet boots and socks they had been wearing since the boat arrived at Fellowship Farm.

It was a wonderful relief to take off their wet gumboots and soggy socks, and slip on some warm dry footwear. Together with other children from Kellyton, they then searched through the piles of children's clothes until they each had a warm set of clothes, as well as hats, woolly gloves and scarves. They put their wet boots and socks, and their other dirty clothes into plastic bags, and left them by their beds.

In the classroom next door to the room with the clothes, there were games and toys for children of all ages. There was even an old guitar and some other instruments that had also been donated. There were children playing with Lego, while others drew. Some were playing cards, and Leezah could see some of her classmates setting up a game of dominos. The Fitzgerald children went over and asked if they could join in.

After a few games of dominos, the children noticed some delicious cooking smells coming from the undercover area outside. They wandered outside and saw that, under bright electric lights a hot dinner was being prepared for serving. There were long rows of heated silver-coloured trays containing rice, stews, soup, vegetables and other food.

"Yum!" said Olingah as his tummy rumbled loudly.

One of the older men setting up the tables gave him a big smile. "Dinner will be ready in about ten minutes son."

"Thanks!" said Olingah.

The children went back inside to look for their parents. Flip and Rommy were talking to Colby near their beds. As the children approached, Flip, Rommy and Colby greeted them. "Have you finished rescuing everyone?" asked Skye-Maree.

"Aye," said Colby, with a big wink and a nod. "All rescued!"

"Dinner is going to be ready in ten minutes!" said Olingah.

"Great!" said Rommy, Flip, and Colby all at once. The children weren't the only ones who were hungry.

"Would you like to eat with us?" asked Rommy.

"That would be great," replied Colby. "I have a question for the wee bairns here."

"Bairns?" asked Leezah.

"He means midgets, children, you," explained Flip.

As they walked outside together and lined up to get a plate and some food, Colby asked the children: "What is it that you know then?"

The children looked puzzled.

"What is that you know that makes you different?"

"Different?" asked Leezah. "Different, how?"

"Today I met about 25 families," Colby explained. "All of them needed rescuing. All of them had their houses flooded. All of them were cold and hungry. But you were the only family who met us with smiles as wide as the Sydney Harbour Bridge! You were the only ones who didn't mention even once that your carpet and furniture got wrecked by the flood. You were the only ones who were worried about the wildlife, and the only children who said 'thank you' when we arrived at the bus. So why are you different?"

"Bahá'u'lláh," said Skye-Maree.

"Behoolala?" replied Colby, looking surprised.

Skye-Maree was about to explain, when Colby got called away by one of the other volunteers.

"I'll have to take a rain check on this conversation," he apologised. "Pardon the pun!"

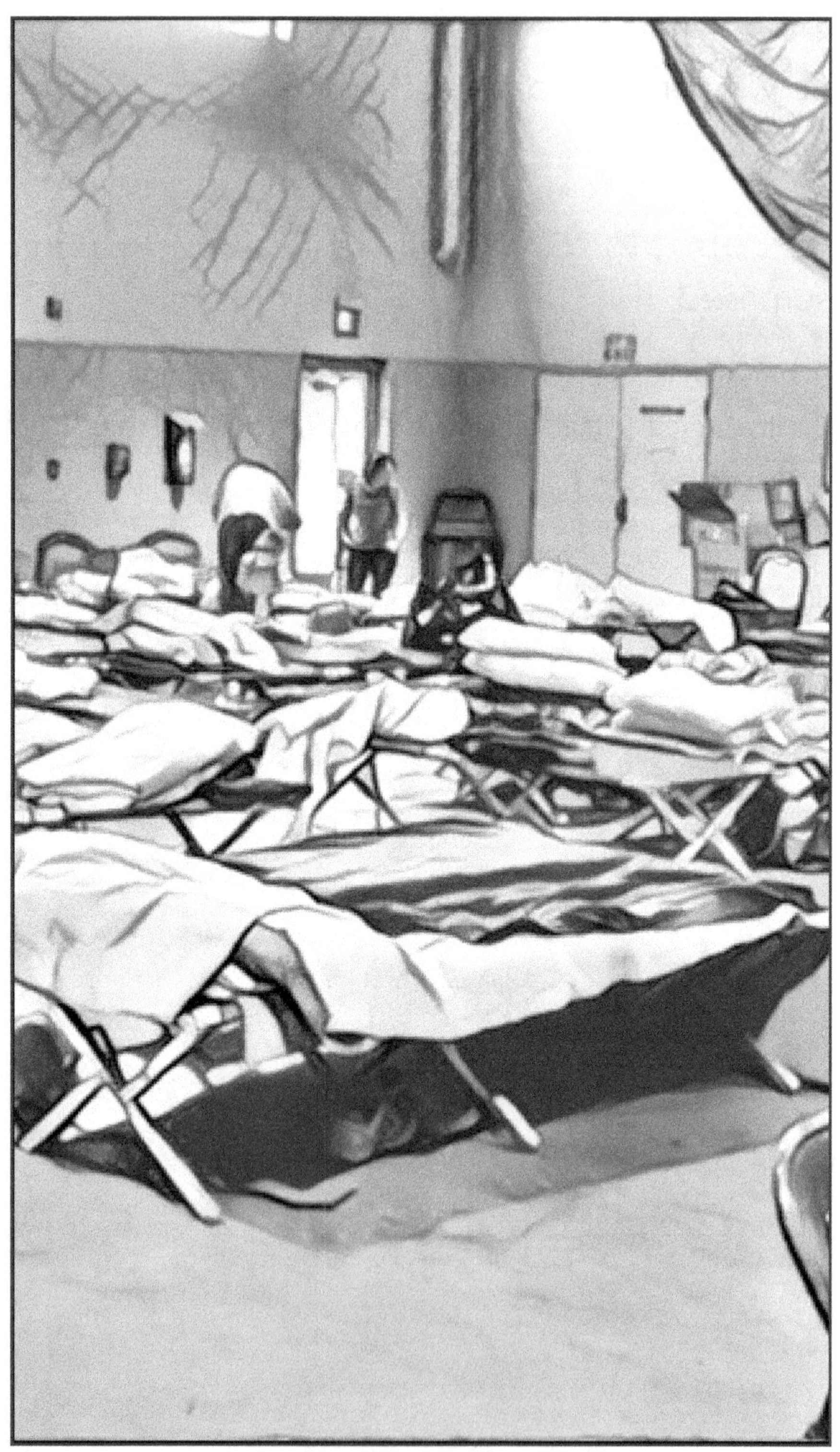

Thankful in adversity

Just before coming out to dinner, Rommy had taken her phone off charge. She turned it on as they waited in the line. Ping. Ping. Ping. Ping. Lots of messages were coming through one after the other. "It's Uncle Jack, Aunty Jen, Grandma and Grandpa! They are all wondering if we are ok. The Kellyton floods were on the news." Rommy sent the family a text to let them know everyone was safe and well, and promised to call later.

Dinner was absolutely delicious! Everyone was ravenous, and there were lots of different tasty foods to choose from. And there was even dessert: Hot custard and fruit cake. After dinner a new team of volunteers arrived and the first team went to have some rest.

They handed out packs with toothbrushes, toothpaste, soap and small towels. There were no showers at the evacuation centre, but the school toilets were open so the sinks and toilets could be used. It felt strange to be brushing their teeth in a school toilet block.

After they had brushed their teeth, Leezah brought the guitar out of the play room and passed it to Flip.

"Great idea!' exclaimed Flip. "Let's sing some songs before we have our prayers." Many of the Kellyton children had attended Holy Days, or Ayyám-i-Há, or children's classes at Fellowship Farm at some time or another.

When they saw the Fitzgerald family settling in to sing some songs, many of them gathered around. This attracted the attention of others, and soon there were many children and families gathered around the Fitzgerald family. Flip started off with a song that was easy to learn.

"We are drops!" he sang.

"We are drops," the children echoed.

"Of one ocean," Flip sang.

"Of one ocean," the children echoed.

"We are leaves."

"We are leaves."

"Of one tree."

"Of one tree."

"Come and join us."

"Come and join us."

"In our quest for unity," everyone joined in together, "It's a way of life for you and me!"

"Bravo bravo!" cried Flip before leading everyone into the second verse.

The singing made all the children feel light and happy. Even the worried parents were able to relax a little and enjoy the music. Somehow the songs with their joyful lyrics helped everyone feel a little more grateful, and a little less worried. No-one from Kellyton had been injured in the flood, and even the pets were all safe, dry, and had full bellies.

After many many songs, Flip invited the large group of Kellyton residents to join them for some prayers. The Fitzgerald family started to sing, "Blessed is the spot, and the house, and the place…" They sang a few more prayers and some Hidden Words.

When they finished, everyone clapped. Leezah, Skye-Maree and Olingah felt embarrassed that their friends were clapping after prayers. They also knew that their friends just wanted to show appreciation for the beautiful prayers and music.

Although Colby's volunteer shift had finished after dinner, he had stayed for the music and prayers. He wanted to continue the conversation that was interrupted earlier. As the other friends called out good night and headed to their own beds on the floor of the gym, Colby came over and sat next to Flip on the edge of Skye-Maree's bed.

"So you were saying Bahloolala is your magic potion?"

"Ba-ha-u-llah," said Skye-Maree slowly and clearly. "We are Bahá'ís."

"Oh! Bahá'ís. I had a Bahá'í professor when I was at university in Hobart," said Colby. "He invited all the students to join in something he called 'devotional meetings' on campus, and other things too."

"My uncle teaches at a university in Hobart. What was your professor's name?" asked Skye-Maree.

"I think it was Dr Campbell-something. He taught peace-building," replied Colby.

"That's Uncle Jack!" exclaimed Skye-Maree.

"No way?"

Skye-Maree nodded vigorously.

"Well, I have to say, I never went to anything he invited us to. I just ignored him. I just thought he was a weirdo."

"Oh, he is a weirdo," said Flip with a serious face. "But that's got nothing to do with Bahá'u'lláh."

"Well I'd like to hear more about whatever magic potion Bahá'u'lláh is offering! And I really liked the songs you sang tonight. I'm exhausted now, but I'll be back tomorrow. I hope we get a chance to talk some more."

"We should definitely do that," said Flip. "It's funny because Skye's name is linked to a place that is special for you. And your name is linked to a person that is special for Bahá'ís."

Colby's eyebrows shot up. "Really? Well now I'm intrigued. I'll be hunting you out tomorrow for sure!"

At eight o'clock the bright lights in the gym were turned out, so children and others who wanted to sleep could sleep. The hall was still lit by lamps placed along the walls so it still wasn't really dark. Rommy left the gym and went into the play room to talk to the family members who had made contact earlier. Flip settled the children for sleep.

"Daddy, when will we be able to go back to the farm?" asked Skye-Maree.

"We will be able to go back when the flood waters go down," replied Flip.

"How long do you think that will be?"

"Well, it seems to have stopped raining, so maybe tomorrow or the next day. I'm not sure."

"Will our house be okay?"

"Our house will be wet and muddy, and there might not be clean water in the taps, and their might even be some nice surprises out of the toilet floating around."

"YUK!" cried Leezah.

"Yep! It might take us a while to clean up," said Flip.

"Where will we live while we clean up?" asked Olingah.

"I'm not sure," replied Flip. "We'll consult about that tomorrow." Flip stroked Olingah's head with his hand, soothingly. Just as Olingah was heading off to sleep, Flip said quietly, "Did you see what happened my little sonshine?" Olingah shook his head sleepily.

"Our farm and house got flooded. We didn't have much to eat for a while. We have had to practice flexibility and patience, but Bahá'u'lláh gave us all the strength we needed."

Olingah nodded sleepily.

"Bahá'u'lláh might send all sorts of things to us. Some might call them 'bad' things, or difficult things. But we can trust that He will always give us the strength we need to be 'generous in prosperity and thankful in adversity'.

Olingah nodded, right off to sleep.

If the children had known what the morning was going to bring, none of them would have been able to sleep. They would have been running in circles, doing cartwheels and yelling yippee!! But that is another story!

THE END

Images

Book 13: 1 travelcedric @ Flickr; 2 Dinner-to-be @ Flickr; 3 Ruha Fifita; 4 @ pxhere.com; 5 home made; 6 Gaspard Maynés @ pexels.com; 7 Maksym Kozlenko @ Wikimedia Commons; 8 ; @ goodfreephotos.com; 9 @ sphere.com; 10 @ pixabay.com

Book 14: 1 Cory Doctorow @ Flick; 2 BlueMix @ pixabay.com; 3 Gellinger @ pixabay.com; 4 @ pexels.com; 5 hzv_westfalen_de @ pixabay.com; 6 calflier001 @ Wikimedia Commons; 7 Air National Guard; 8 @ pxhere.com; 9 James Gathany @ Wikimedia Commons

Book 15: 1 @ Wikimedia Commons; 2 SpokaneWilly @ Wikimedia Commons; 3 Meditations @ pixabay.com; 4 Adam.J.W.C. @ Wikimedia Commons; 5 Daniel Case @ Wikimedia Commons; 6 @ Wikimedia Commons; 7 Plamen Agov @ Wikimedia Commons; 8 Lyle Radford @ Wikimedia Commons; 9 Eitan f @ Wikimedia Commons; 10 George Armstrong @ Wikimedia Commons

Michelangela

website - www.michelangela.com.au
email - info@michelangela.com.au

To receive Michelangela's occasional
product announcements
please visit our website to subscribe.

Unity in Diversity series

This brightly illustrated picture book contains five simple stories for young readers. They foster an understanding of the oneness of the human race and celebrate its diversity within that unity.

Likening the human race to various coloured cotton in a woven cloth, various fruits on the tree of life, stars in the heavens, members of one body, and different notes in one perfect chord, the stories use the concrete to teach the abstract.

Young readers will enjoy the bright colours and simple text as they develop their understanding of the unity and diversity of the human race.

Ideal for children aged 4-8 years.

Order online from reputable retailers, or digitally from the iBookstore. Also available as read-to-me stories in English, from the iBookstore. Also available as individual stories on premium paper, softcover and hardcover.

Translated into French, Portuguese, Romanian, Tetum, and Mongolian.

Crowned Heart series

The *Crowned Heart* series is the popular and inspiring collection of stories for young readers, drawn from Lights of Fortitude. It introduces three beloved heroines of the Faith.

"How many queens of the world have laid down their heads on a pillow of dust and disappeared... Not so the handmaids who ministered at the Threshold of God; these have shone forth like glittering stars in the skies of ancient glory, shedding their splendors across all the reaches of time." - `Abdu'l-Bahá.

These are the stories of Hand of the Cause of God, Martha Root, Clara Dunn and Corrine True. These easy to read stories are accompanied by truly exquisite watercolor illustrations by Katayoun Mottahedin.

Enjoyable reading for children 4-8 years of age.

Available in softcover and hardcover on premium paper. Order online from reputable retailers, or digitally from the iBookstore.

Fellowship Farm series

Leezah, Skye-Maree and Olingah Fitzgerald live with their parents on Fellowship Farm. In the first book of the *Fellowship Farm series*, you will meet the children and learn about their daily activities on the farm.

There is a lot to be done each day: pillow fights, morning prayers, pig feeding and school bus riding.They help their dad feed the cows, add stickers to their virtues poster and learn to deal with bullies.

Then you will join the Fitzgerald children on their many adventures with puppies, snake bites, treasure hunts, bonfires, camping by the sea, and tree houses. And as they go they sometimes practice their virtues, and sometimes forget...

Five volumes in the series, covering books 1-15.

Suitable for independent readers aged 8-12 years; parent-read from six years.

Order online from reputable retailers, or digitally from the iBookstore or Kindle store.

Reflections on Reality series

This is the first book in the *Reflections on Reality* series.

The Big Story explains the way in which the divinely ordained and guided process that has brought human beings into existence has taken place gradually over time and space. It shows that the concepts of evolution and creation are not mutually exclusive.

Science and religion are shown to be two windows on one reality, two knowledge systems that when properly understood, function as one cohesive whole.

Suitable for independent readers aged 14+ years; with assistance from 12+.

Order online from reputable retailers, or digitally from the iBookstore.

The Divine Plan

This is the second book in the *Reflections on Reality* series.

Building on the foundation laid in the first book of the series, *The Divine Plan* examines social and cultural maturation throughout history.

The impetus provided by the Manifestations of God for this maturation is explored, as are the disintegrative and integrative forces at play in society today. It describes the opportunities, unique to this period of human history, available to the individual and the collective, to develop latent capacities essential to the establishment of a divine civilisation.

Suitable for independent readers aged 14+ years.

Order online from reputable retailers, or digitally from the iBookstore.

www.ingramcontent.com/pod-product-compliance
Lightning Source LLC
Chambersburg PA
CBHW061019120726
47910CB00006B/2022